PRAISE FOR

Haunting Jasmine

"The kind of book that makes me remember all the reasons I love to read. Anjali Banerjee writes in luminous prose about the deepest secrets of a woman's heart. With a freshness of voice and a playfulness of the imagination, she brings her quirky characters to life. The gorgeous and multilayered language illuminates a story that will haunt the reader long after the final page is turned."

—Susan Wiggs, *New York Times* bestselling author

"Part love story, part ghost story, and all in all a thoroughly entertaining tale that will leave readers happy and satisfied by the surprising end. Banerjee intertwines traditions of her Bengali ancestry throughout the story, giving the tale an exotic twist that is as spicy and comforting as the delicious Indian dishes that are so appetizingly described. This is a book destined to become a perennial favorite with romance readers as well as fans of otherworldly tales."

—*Las Vegas Review-Journal*

"Banerjee's opulent prose is as colorful as Auntie's cherished keepsakes, and gently ironic supernatural elements . . . add dimension to a romance that spins refreshingly into a quirky, surprising denouement."

—*Publishers Weekly*

"A literary ghost story, a gentle romance, and an homage to the Bengali culture as transplanted to our region. It is a subtle and encouraging book."

—*The Bellingham Herald*

continued . . .

"The recent spate of stories about life in America from the perspective of second-generation immigrants is wonderful, and Banerjee's contribution is a welcome one . . . Jasmine's interactions with the world, and even with the spirit world, are believable. The paranormal aspects of the novel are creative and fun."   —*RT Book Reviews*

FURTHER PRAISE FOR
ANJALI BANERJEE AND HER NOVELS

"Fresh and highly entertaining. I loved every word."
  —Susan Elizabeth Phillips, *New York Times* bestselling author

"A masala-scented *Like Water for Chocolate*."
                                    —*San Francisco Chronicle*

"Delectable . . . recounted with hilarity and warmth."
                                    —*The Seattle Post-Intelligencer*

"This book has a romantic, magical quality."   —*Booklist*

"Fascinating, insightful, and delightful. The descriptions shimmer and sparkle. I intend to rush out and buy a copy for every woman I know."
        —Jayne Ann Krentz, *New York Times* bestselling author

"The author's hip-hot style combines breezy storytelling, wry humor, and just enough poignant sauce in a romantic comedy equal to *Bend It Like Beckham*."   —*The Seattle Times*

"A *Bridget Jones's Diary* meets *Monsoon Wedding*–style escapade."
                                    —*Publishers Weekly*

Titles by Anjali Banerjee

HAUNTING JASMINE

ENCHANTING LILY

Enchanting Lily

ANJALI BANERJEE

BERKLEY BOOKS, NEW YORK

THE BERKLEY PUBLISHING GROUP
Published by the Penguin Group
Penguin Group (USA) Inc.
375 Hudson Street, New York, New York 10014, USA
Penguin Group (Canada), 90 Eglinton Avenue East, Suite 700, Toronto, Ontario M4P 2Y3, Canada
(a division of Pearson Penguin Canada Inc.) • Penguin Books Ltd., 80 Strand, London WC2R 0RL,
England • Penguin Group Ireland, 25 St. Stephen's Green, Dublin 2, Ireland (a division of Penguin
Books Ltd.) • Penguin Group (Australia), 250 Camberwell Road, Camberwell, Victoria 3124, Australia
(a division of Pearson Australia Group Pty. Ltd.) • Penguin Books India Pvt. Ltd., 11 Community
Centre, Panchsheel Park, New Delhi—110 017, India • Penguin Group (NZ), 67 Apollo Drive,
Rosedale, Auckland 0632, New Zealand (a division of Pearson New Zealand Ltd.) • Penguin Books
(South Africa) (Pty.) Ltd., 24 Sturdee Avenue, Rosebank, Johannesburg 2196, South Africa

Penguin Books Ltd., Registered Offices: 80 Strand, London WC2R 0RL, England

This book is an original publication of The Berkley Publishing Group.

This is a work of fiction. Names, characters, places, and incidents either are the product of the author's
imagination or are used fictitiously, and any resemblance to actual persons, living or dead, business
establishments, events, or locales is entirely coincidental. The publisher does not have any control over
and does not assume any responsibility for author or third-party websites or their content.

Copyright © 2012 by Anjali Banerjee.
Excerpt from *Haunting Jasmine* copyright © 2010 by Anjali Banerjee.
Cover design by Laura Drew Design.
Cover photo by Shutterstock.
Text design by Kristin del Rosario.

PUBLISHING HISTORY
Berkley trade paperback edition / August 2012

Library of Congress Cataloging-in-Publication Data

Banerjee, Anjali.
Enchanting Lily / Anjali Banerjee.
p. cm.
ISBN 978-0-425-24530-9 (pbk.)
1. Widows—Fiction. 2. Northwest, Pacific—Fiction. I. Title.
PS3602.A6355E53 2012
813'.6—dc23
2011046325

PRINTED IN THE UNITED STATES OF AMERICA

10 9 8 7 6 5 4 3 2 1

In memory of
Andrei I. Bazdyrev and Byron Sacre

The past scampers like an alley cat through the present, leaving the paw prints of memories scattered helter-skelter.

—CHARLES DE LINT, *The Onion Girl*

Chapter One

Kitty

This morning, I take my usual route to the Fairport Inn for breakfast, enjoying the sweet smells of autumn leaves, salty ocean, and exquisite wild salmon. Here on our misty island, the day is beginning to hum. Quaint shops are opening their doors; proprietors are setting up hand-painted signs on the sidewalks. Chickadees and juncos flit in the nearby trees. As always, I take the shortcut through the overgrown yard of a yellow cottage, the empty one with a sign in front, but this time I stop for a closer look.

I sense that someone will soon arrive on the ferry from

Seattle, someone who belongs in the cottage, someone who needs me. On this island, she will seek her own island, a small castle of loneliness away from the world. It won't be long now, so I crouch in the garden to wait.

Lily

Lily drove north from San Francisco in search of a dream. The farther she traveled, the more the possibilities unfurled before her. She began to envision a future beyond the heaviness of loss, and yet she could still feel her husband, Josh, sitting next to her, a faint reminder of the life she was leaving behind. On this route, he would've planned each detour, each stop, each hotel. She imagined his head bent forward over a crinkled map, making sure they stayed on track.

But now she could do anything she wanted. She could lose her way. She could take a dirt road on a whim. She could disappear and nobody would know. She relished this new freedom, and yet she felt unmoored, anonymous. Who would care if she veered off a cliff? Her body might lie at the bottom of a ravine, decaying for weeks before anyone found her. The truck would rust and eventually fall apart.

She wondered if she had become invisible, a solitary young widow without community or connections, heading toward an uncertain fate. The farthest north she'd ever been was Seattle—she and Josh had taken a plane. The captain had pointed out Crater Lake, Mount Saint Helens, and Mount Rainier, all tiny and manageable from a height of thirty thousand feet.

But this time, Lily stuck to the road, the terrain rushing by in life-sized color. She raced through the flat agricultural fields of central California, stopped to hike in the cool shadows of the redwood trees near the Oregon border. She took comfort in knowing that this ancient forest had existed virtually unchanged for millions of years; that it would likely remain long after her death. There was something immense and unknowable in nature, a mysterious truth that put her grief in perspective.

As she navigated the steep mountain highways of southern Oregon, she thought Josh would've loved the breathtaking views of Mount Shasta, the descent into the lush valleys, the density of firs. No longer bound by the material world, he could follow her into restaurants and parks, rest stops and motel rooms. He was everywhere and nowhere.

In an Ashland hotel, late at night, she awoke to his breath on her cheek. But when she turned over, she touched only the pillow, and the familiar pain settled into her chest. How could she do this alone? An experience had never seemed real unless she shared it with Josh. Had her existence become ephemeral? She half expected to lose her concrete sense of self, to become a fog that drifted across the planet.

Where was she going? When did she plan to stop? She sought the perfect destination, the kind of idyllic getaway that she and Josh had often discussed. She would know the town when she saw it, and she figured the Toyota Tacoma could reliably carry her there, even with the trailer hitched to the back. Inside the cargo space, she'd packed her most precious possessions, the ones she couldn't bring herself to sell at the estate sale: Josh's best costume creations and the dozens of vintage treasures she'd collected over the years, from Chanel pullovers to Halston dresses, Escada purses to rhinestone jewelry.

The truck and trailer carried her all the way to Seattle and then on the ferry to Shelter Island, a green dot of rain-soaked darkness in the middle of the Puget Sound. She expected to drive through wilderness and catch another boat and then another, but as she descended the ramp into the quaint town of Fairport, the island's main community, a peculiar thing happened. Time slowed. A silver mist crept in from the ocean, gradually clearing to reveal cast-iron lampposts lining the waterfront road, giant old pop-lar trees, and moss growing through cracks in the redbrick sidewalks. Rose and lavender bushes swayed in a soft autumn breeze. Slanted sunlight lent an otherworldly glow to the rows of tiny shops, each nestled in an antique brick building or converted Craftsman-style cottage.

She drove past Island Eye Care, Classic Cycle, Le Pichet Restaurant, and Jasmine's Bookstore perched on a hillside in a burnt umber and white Victorian.

Josh would've appreciated this old-world charm—islanders strolling along at a leisurely pace, enjoying a pris-tine morning. A woman in a tight blue jogging suit walked her golden retriever, the dog stopping to mark every lamp-post. A white-haired couple strolled along, looking in windows, slurping from coffee cups. That was what Lily needed—caffeine.

She parked on Harborside Road and bought a mocha at the Java Hut, a warm shop in which watercolor paint-ings of the ocean and mountains adorned the walls. Locals in flannel shirts, jeans, and knit caps chatted at small tables, and the smells of coffee and baked goods swirled in the air. She imagined sitting by the window and reading for hours.

The barista, a handsome teenager with blue-black hair, lean muscle pulling at his T-shirt, and a tattoo of an anchor on his neck, gave her a friendly smile and put a chocolate espresso bean on the lid of her cup.

"The magic bean," he said, handing her the paper cup.

The chocolate was beginning to melt on the lid. "What does it do?" she asked. "Does it grow a beanstalk?"

"You eat the bean, and anything can happen. Your wildest dreams fulfilled." He gave her a few quarters in change, which she dropped into the tip jar.

"I'm not sure I have a wildest dream." Maybe she could eat the bean and Josh would materialize, alive and well.

"Come on, everyone does. Eat it and make a wish."

"Tall order for a tiny bean, don't you think? Fulfilling a grand, impossible wish?"

He draped a dish towel over his shoulder. "Hey, there's no such thing as impossible. You're not from around here, are you?"

"I guess it's obvious." She felt her face flushing, and she instinctively patted her hair, although she could easily have been the boy's mother. What did she look like to him? Disheveled and crazy, probably. An almost forty-year-old woman with crow's-feet and a wild, wavy mane streaked with gray. Full lips, smudged mascara. She wasn't fashionable in her travel clothes—wrinkled sweater, faded jeans, and running shoes. Who could know that she harbored vintage Sue Wong and Valentino in the trailer?

He tilted his head to the side. "You just have the visitor kind of look. Enjoy your stay!" He turned to the next customer, a husky man in a rain jacket. The tide of noise rushed in—laughter, the buzz of conversation, the click of laptop keys.

She hurried out to the truck and sat in the driver's seat, not starting the engine. In the rearview mirror, she tried to see what had given her away. She detected no obvious signs on her face. Maybe it was just that everyone knew everyone here, but nobody knew *her*.

She ate the crunchy, bitter coffee bean and licked the sweet, melted chocolate off her fingers. Feeling a bit silly, she waited a moment for the magic to take effect, but nothing happened. So she started the truck and pulled out into the empty street. How relaxing, she thought, not to worry about traffic.

She'd nearly reached the end of Harborside Road when she saw it—a Victorian cottage the color of churned butter, with white shutters, blue porch, brick chimney, and cracked sidewalk leading up through an overgrown yard. A Fairport Realty sign read *For Sale, Residential/Commercial.*

As she parked at the curb, her heartbeat kicked up. This was it—the cottage of her imagination. She pictured vintage black dresses on a carousel, jewelry in a glass case, silk scarves displayed on an antique table. But perhaps someone had already tried opening a shop and had failed—hence the empty rooms and neglected garden. She thought she saw a white cat crouched in the grass, but when she parked and got out of the truck, the cat had disappeared.

She traipsed through the yard and peered into the windows. On the downstairs level were two front rooms, sparsely furnished with an antique red armchair, a rugged oak table. The walls were cream-colored with pale blue trim and painted ivy vines. Blue! Josh's favorite color. A wide hallway led back to a narrow kitchen. The floors were a dark burnished hardwood.

She walked around the house to peer into the kitchen window. The previous tenants had left behind a pine breakfast nook and stainless-steel appliances. Josh had loved stainless steel. She could move in immediately, and she would have a place to sit while waiting for the furniture to arrive from storage.

Too soon to think this way, the practical side of her warned. *One step at a time.* In the back, a gravel path wound through weedy flowerbeds to a ramshackle shed. A lone, majestic maple tree grew in the center of the garden, dropping yellow leaves in a fairy ring around its base. On either side of the property, tall privet hedges formed a privacy barrier between the house and the shops next door. On the right, in an old brick building, Island Creamery sold handmade ice cream in sugar cones. On the left, in a gray Victorian, Apothecary Shop carried a hodgepodge of touristy items displayed in stained glass windows. Across the street, the sign for a small, modern clothing store swung in the wind: *The Newest Thing.*

Maybe it wouldn't be wise to open another boutique right across the street, but how could she resist the charm of this little yellow cottage? She imagined that on the attic level, she would find two bedrooms with slanted ceilings and perhaps a bathroom in between. She would sleep up there and sell clothes downstairs. But a moment later, sudden fright overtook her. Here she was, a single woman in a strange town on a remote island, with limited funds and a trailer filled with dusty remnants of a past life. What did she think she was doing? *Okay, breathe. In and out through the nose.*

What price was the owner asking? What would it cost to set up shop? She needed fixtures, a computer system, a loan. What if she failed? *One step at a time.*

A robin took off from the garden, a worm in its beak, and overhead a bald eagle soared, spreading its magnificent wings, and Lily felt Josh beside her. He didn't speak, didn't give her a sign, but she turned on her cell phone anyway and punched in the number for Fairport Realty. What would she say? *Hello, I'm a wandering young widow looking for a home. And by the way, can I move in tonight?*

A perky female voice came on the line. "Fairport Realty, Paige speaking. How may I help you?"

"Paige Williams? Your name is on the sign in front of this house on Harborside Road. The one for sale?"

"Oh, you mean the candy cottage!"

"I don't know—it is yellow. I'm Lily Byrne. I was passing through town, and I'd like to—"

"Are you there right now? If you're there, I'll swing on by. I'm only a block away. Everything is within walking distance in our little town."

A Paul Simon song popped into her head. *In my little town . . . and after it rains there's a rainbow and all of the colors are black.*

"Um, yes, I'm here right now. I'll wait."

"I'll be there in a few."

Lily hung up and paced, suddenly noticing tiny flaws in the house—a bit of peeling plaster here, a bare spot there, a hairline crack in the foundation. And no garage. She would have to buy a tarp or carport, as Josh had treasured his truck. He would not want his precious baby exposed to the elements. In the city, they'd shared a parking garage with other condominium owners.

But even without the garage, the cottage felt right—and almost palatial compared to the condo. In San Francisco, who but the ultra-rich could afford a big house? She and Josh hadn't minded the lack of space. They'd loved being practically on top of each other. Their honeymoon period had lasted through their entire marriage. They were perpetually like two giddy newlyweds gazing into each other's eyes. Joshua's eyes—green flecked with hazel, alive and intelligent.

I wish I could show you this cottage, the view, the sun trapped in pools of light on the waves. He would've loved this small town, woven into the fabric of the forest and sitting right next to the ocean. Already she was thinking as if she lived here, and she hadn't even been inside the house.

Sometimes you just know, Josh had once said when he'd bought an expensive coat on impulse. *You do it and don't think too much.*

But buying a cottage was not the same as buying a coat. Or was it? She traipsed around to the back again, this time noticing new features in the yard—an empty wooden squirrel house nailed to the old shed, a broken ceramic birdbath lying in what had once been a raised flower bed. Faded nursery tags lay here and there, a few still attached to plants. One tag on a bush with bright red flowers read "Salvia Hot Lips, sustainably grown." On the back of the tag were the words "Salvia microphylla. Stunning red and white flowers bloom all summer." The plant had defied the odds and still bloomed in autumn.

"Are you Lily?" a perky voice said behind her.

Lily turned to find a fresh-faced woman striding toward her in a brown sweater and boots, floral frock and leggings, bouncy blonde curls and a blinding sunshine smile. "Yes, I'm Lily. You startled me. You must be Paige."

"Sorry. I tend to sneak up on people."

"Thanks for coming out on short notice."

"It was such a long trek from around the corner. The owner has been trying to lease this place for a while now. Maybe I shouldn't say that. But what the heck. It's the economy. Who can resist such a cute little cottage?" Her dangling gold earrings glinted in the light. But her eyes— dazzling blue—suggested some hidden layer of pain.

"It's beautiful," Lily said, nodding. "I can see the possibilities. Something drew me to it."

"Must be our mystical island." Paige reached out to shake Lily's hand, her fingers firm and bejeweled. But no wedding ring. Was she divorced, engaged, or unmarried?

"So I hear. The barista at the Java Hut gave me a magic coffee bean," Lily said, and laughed.

"Oh yeah, those coffee beans will make you bold."

"I guess this one did!" Was Paige serious? Did everyone in this town believe in the mystical island of magic coffee beans?

"Come on in," Paige said, heading up the front steps.

She pulled a ring of keys from her purse and opened the front door. Her fingers trembled a little. Inside, the cottage was unusually warm and smelled of furniture polish and paint. The wood floor creaked beneath her feet. A house that made noises. A house that lived.

As they walked through the rooms, Paige kept talking in a nervous chatter. "So a retired couple decided to open a candy store in here for a while, which is why I called it the candy cottage. Before that it was a soap depot. You know, all kinds of expensive toiletries and fragrances, spritzers and lotions and stuff—but I'm sorry to say neither business survived."

"Maybe the cottage was waiting for the perfect buyer."

"You're probably right." Paige played with the strap of her oversized shoulder bag. "Someone who appreciates the town's historic qualities, right? Speaking of which, I'm on the board of the Renewal Society. We're dedicated to putting our unique heritage to work for economic growth. Oops, I sound like a commercial. But each of us wears more than one hat around here. It's tough. Sometimes I think I'll pack it all in and move, but I love the island so I stay."

"I don't blame you." Lily peeked into the downstairs half bathroom, which had also been remodeled. "This place is charming."

"I think it was built around 1904. We've got many houses on the list of historic landmarks. The Fairport Art Gallery used to be the first mill site during the Klondike Gold Rush, and Le Pichet belonged to an undertaker. When he moved here, he found everyone was so healthy, they didn't need his services. Like nobody ever died, right? He ended up opening a furniture store instead, and then the building went through a bunch of changes and eventually became a restaurant."

Lily nodded politely, picturing herself ensconced here in peace and quiet. No chatter, no city sounds, no intrusions, no reminders. Just a little house. She touched the freshly painted trim on the arched doorway from the front room to the dining area. Both rooms could hold a few racks of clothing. The room to the right of the entryway could be for shoes, ties, and hats.

"Do you want to see the upper level?" Paige said, but Lily was already heading to the staircase. Paige hurried to follow her.

The two bedrooms were prettier than Lily had imagined—luminescent, with slanted ceilings, big windows, and fresh white paint with blue trim. A bright bathroom sat between them, a new claw-foot tub in the center. A tub! She could take endless bubble baths in peace.

"This is perfect," she said. "Exactly what I've been

looking for." What was she saying? What if the pipes leaked? What if the attic was full of mold?

As if reading her mind, Paige said, "I'm sure the owner could answer any questions you might have or address any concerns—"

"That would be great." Lily sat on the single bed. Firm mattress, unyielding, but fine for now. Otherwise she could unroll her sleeping bag on the floor. She would avoid the double bed in the other room. Too much empty space. "Is the owner nearby? I'd like to talk to him."

"Her." Paige smiled. "We could go over there. You would live here with your whole family then?"

"I don't have a family. I'm it."

A pause. "I see. Okay, that's fine. Probably good—"

"Can we go right now? Is the owner around?" What was she getting herself into? She was already imagining a bedspread to match the walls; a plant in the window. Lavender soap on the bathroom sink. Maybe the magic coffee bean was working after all.

Chapter Two

Lily

"I should warn you about the owner," Paige said on the walk through town. Lily was happy to stretch her legs, to breathe in the clean, salty island air.

"Oh?" she replied. "Is she eccentric?"

"Not her, exactly, but her bookstore. You think the magic coffee bean thing is weird? Jasmine's Bookstore is a bit unusual. Not like your typical bookstore."

"So the owner runs a bookstore. How funny." Lily couldn't imagine what a "typical" bookstore looked like. In her experience, each one had a different personality—

quaint and packed with rare tomes, or spacious and corporate, or musty and dark.

"Jasmine's got this weird sixth sense about books," Paige said, keeping to the redbrick sidewalk, nodding here and there to an occasional passerby, people she obviously knew. "She handed me a paperback about the history of the island once. Got me interested in restoration, so I joined the Renewal Society, and that's how I found out my husband was cheating on me."

"Oh no! Because of the book?"

"Without it, I never would've joined the Society, and I wouldn't have found out."

A bit of a stretch, Lily thought, but possible. "Did you catch him in the act?"

"Not exactly, but close enough. John told me he was singing on Tuesday nights. The Sailor Singers meet in the building right next to the museum, where the Renewal Society meets. He'd started going on Tuesdays and Thursdays, and I thought, that's a lot of singing. But when I stopped in, he wasn't there. He hadn't been there in a while. I pestered one of the guys and he finally spilled the beans. Oops, there I go, mentioning beans again."

"I'm so sorry that happened to you. How long were you married?"

"Seven years. The divorce wasn't all his fault. I have

some . . . regrets. Oh, look, there it is." She pointed at the burnt umber and white Victorian perched on a hillside overlooking the water.

Lily felt like the house watched her, but not unkindly. Large bay windows reflected silvery light, and the words "Jasmine's Bookstore" glittered on a garden sign in bright gold lettering. "It does look enchanted," she said.

"See what I mean?" Paige headed up the walkway to the door. "Mystical, huh?"

"Like it stepped out of another era."

Paige opened the door and ushered Lily into the foyer. "This used to be the back servants' entrance during the height of the timber industry. The front entrance faces the waterfront. At one time, all the important guests arrived by sea."

"Hard to imagine a world without cars." Lily pictured wooden sailboats gliding into the harbor, horse-drawn carriages rattling down cobblestone streets.

"Must've been a better time, if you ask me."

"Maybe." Inside the bookstore, soft lights from Tiffany lamps spilled out across Persian carpets, and here and there, portraits of famous authors adorned the walls—Shakespeare, Virginia Woolf, Mark Twain, and others. Muffled voices drifted from nearby rooms, and the smells of old house—of dust and oak and paper—rose and mixed with a fresh citrus scent of potpourri. To the left stood a three-foot-tall brass statue of the Hindu elephant-headed god, Ganesh. Lily had seen various versions of him inside Indian restaurants and shops in San Francisco. His smiling face, rotund belly, and large feet were an anomaly in this old Victorian mansion—the flavor of India in the Pacific Northwest. But then, her shop would be an anomaly, too. Who would imagine theater costumes and the best of haute couture fashion for sale in a sleepy island town?

"You have to touch his feet!" Paige whispered. "You have to honor the god of new beginnings."

Lily bent to touch the statue's pudgy brass feet. "Am I supposed to pray or something?"

"Whatever you want. But don't tell me or you'll jinx it."

Lily closed her eyes and asked the elephant god to help her find a way forward. She didn't dare ask for Josh, although she longed for him. But she'd read a story about a woman who asked for her husband back, and he returned all mangled, in the form in which he had died. There were consequences when you wished for the impossible. So she swallowed her yearning, just as an ethereal-looking woman emerged from the parlor, a vision of beauty in blue jeans and a cherry sweater, wavy black hair falling past her shoulders. Her cheeks glowed with happiness. An engraved gold wedding band glinted on her ring finger, and Lily felt an unwelcome stab of envy. She couldn't remember when she'd felt so happy. Well, she remembered when, but it had been a lifetime ago.

"That was a fast walk over here," the woman said, reaching out to shake Lily's hand. "Paige called and told me you were coming."

Lily nodded, unable to speak.

"I'm Jasmine. Come into the parlor." She ushered Paige and Lily into a large drawing room lined with bookshelves from floor to ceiling and a large bay window.

"Lily is interested in the candy cottage," Paige said, sitting on a plush antique couch. She crossed her legs and swung one booted foot back and forth.

Jasmine gestured toward an ornate Louis XV armchair. "Why don't you have a seat over there?"

Lily had been eyeing that chair. When she sat down, the cushion felt softer than she'd expected. "I should've checked the furnace and electrical system, but my husband was always the one—"

"I understand, don't worry," Jasmine said. "We just rewired the house, if that eases your mind."

It did, a little. "What price are you asking?"

Jasmine named a number that seemed reasonable, but it

would still stretch Lily's finances, and she would still need to take out a loan or two for the business.

"I see." She clasped her hands together in her lap, aware of her bare ring finger, her nails worn to the quick. Since when had she become a nail-biter? "Let me give it some thought."

Jasmine nodded. "I'll just get us some tea and the papers. Maybe you'd like to take another look at the place."

"Thanks, I would." Lily mentally calculated her anticipated expenses and the amount of money she had left. She would need to stay in a hotel for a while, too.

Jasmine left the room, gliding almost as if her feet didn't touch the ground.

"The house used to belong to her aunt," Paige said, lowering her voice. "But the aunt got married and moved back to India."

"Where did Jasmine come from?"

"She had some corporate job in L.A., but the island cast its spell on her, just like it's casting a spell on you."

"The town is certainly charming," Lily said politely. She could hear customers murmuring in other rooms, the sound of pages turning, footsteps. A man sauntered in— solid and broad-shouldered, good-looking in a rugged, roughed-up way. When he noticed Lily and Paige leaning in toward each other, he said, "Oh, sorry," and slipped out into the hall again.

A moment later, Jasmine stepped in with a silver tray of tea and biscuits. She put a manila file folder on the coffee table.

Paige munched and sipped, and Lily took a cup of tea that tasted of peach and lemon. As she settled back in her chair, a rather round, fluffy gray cat waddled into the room and let out a horrendous, grating meow.

"Oh, Mary, I can see you're starving to death," Jasmine said, placing crumbled bits of biscuit on a plate on the floor. "Where's Monet?"

"How many cats do you have?" Lily asked.

"Only two. Monet is about half her size." Jasmine picked up Mary and arranged the gigantic creature in her lap. "She likes to eat, and he likes to wander."

"Ha!" Paige said. "Story of my life."

"I thought I saw a white cat at the cottage," Lily said.

Paige and Jasmine looked at her blankly and shook their heads. Had she actually even seen the cat?

Mary meowed again, jumped off Jasmine's lap, and trotted out of the room.

Jasmine got up, glided to a bookshelf, and extracted a thin hardcover. She handed the book to Lily. "Here's a little welcoming gift. Or a bribe, whatever you want to call it."

"All Buttoned Up," Lily read. *"Poems About Clothing."*

"The title popped out at me."

Paige gave Lily a knowing look.

"Thanks," Lily said. "Very generous of you. I'll pay for it—"

"Not at all!" Jasmine waved her hand.

Lily reached for the manila folder. "Can I borrow this for a while?"

"Of course—take your time."

But even before Lily hired a Realtor and moved into a hotel temporarily, even before the title search on the cottage began; even before she took out a business loan and obtained the correct licenses; even before all that, she knew she would be staying, at least for a while.

Chapter Three

Lily

What was she doing here in her sleeping bag on this single bed in a creaky cottage in the middle of nowhere? No traffic sounds or voices or wind. She couldn't even hear the hum of the refrigerator. Outside, a nearly full moon illuminated the maple tree in the backyard. The branches cast a mottled pattern of shadows and light on the bedroom walls. She felt absurdly like a vagrant squatting in someone else's house, waiting for the true owners to come home and find her asleep in the wrong bed, like Goldilocks.

At least she had electricity, although the telephone was

not yet connected. Her cell phone reception faded in and out, but mostly out. She'd stocked the kitchen cabinets and fridge with basics from Island Organic Grocery, where the checkout clerk had given her a friendly but curious smile. Then she'd wandered through the cottage, opening cabinets and closets and exploring again. She kept repeating to herself that the cottage belonged to her now. The realization both exhilarated and frightened her. She could paint the ceiling any color. She could knock out walls, as long as the roof didn't cave in. What if it did? What would she do? What if the water heater broke or the taps spit out rusty liquid? What if the place was haunted? If it was, she could make friends with the ghosts. She could have tea with them. She could wallpaper the living room with pictures of ghosts. The extent of her freedom gave her a calm, expansive feeling—and yet, there was the nagging loneliness again.

So she'd taken another walk from the downtown area up through sleepy residential streets lined with old Victorians, mainly to become visible to the world again. Occasionally, she'd passed someone working in a garden, and they'd waved at each other. She felt relieved. Someone had seen her. She still had substance. But nobody bothered her, and she preferred to remain at a distance. She'd come back to the cottage pleasantly tired and had spent the last half hour reading through the poems. Until now, she hadn't opened the book.

She landed on a page that shimmered, almost as if the ink were made of crushed silver. The poem was "Ode to the Clothes" by Pablo Neruda. He wrote of becoming one with his clothing, and Lily realized that her comfortable cotton pajamas, with little lighthouses printed on them, had become one with her, too. They'd carried her through the blissful nights with Josh; then through the anguished, sleepless nights following his death; then through the restless nights while she'd dealt with the complicated maze of arrangements—his will, the memorial service, the estate sale. She'd never appreciated the comfort of these pajamas until now.

She closed the book, and she'd just put it on the bedside table and turned off the lamp when she heard a scratching sound, as if a mouse scuttled through the walls. She sat up in the darkness, her heart pounding. Of course, there had to be a drawback to this peaceful abode. Rodents in the walls. She held her breath and listened, but the scratching had stopped.

She let out her breath and lay down again, gazing wide-eyed at the moving shadows on the ceiling. The scratching started again, but distantly, like an animal trying to get in or out of somewhere. What if a raccoon or squirrel had become trapped in that ramshackle shed?

No, the scratching came from downstairs. She got out of bed, put on her robe and slippers, and headed down the wide wooden staircase, sidestepping boxes and turning on lights. Josh had always investigated unusual noises. He'd grabbed a baseball bat that he kept by the nightstand, although he hadn't liked baseball. Had he really expected to whack someone with that thing? Without a violent bone in his body?

Now she felt the weight of her singular responsibility. Rats, mice, bees in the walls. Dealing with the messiness of life was all up to her.

The scratching came from outside the front door, on the porch. She peered out through the peephole but saw nothing. She tried peeking through the front bay window, but she couldn't see onto the porch. What if she opened the door to find a rabid raccoon ready to attack? That's when she heard the meow—a plaintive, piercing sound but unmistakable. A cat.

Instantly Lily thought, *Poor thing, alone out there.* Was it a stray? Feral? Or merely a local resident? Was a predator chasing the cat? Maybe a dog or coyote? Nothing appeared to be moving in the yard, but she knew she would be foolish to open the door. Anything could be waiting in the darkness.

"Go on home!" she called out. "It's the middle of the night." The scratching only became louder and more persistent. Another meow. Maybe the cat was hungry.

Lily rapped gently on the wood, and the scratching stopped. Through the front window, she could see the white cat running down the walkway and disappearing into the bushes. What irresponsible pet owner would let a cat wander at night? She supposed cats were nocturnal. They liked to hunt in the dark, didn't they? But why would this cat scratch at the front door? What if it thought it lived here?

Lily couldn't bear the prospect of going back to bed, knowing an unhappy creature, its stomach probably empty, was crouched in the bushes. If only for her own peace of mind, she rummaged in the kitchen cabinets, found a can of tuna, and dumped its contents on a plate. Then she tiptoed out into the cold night. She'd never seen so many stars crowded into the sky, and the longer she looked, the more abundant they became. A fecundity of stars. The town was quiet except for the soft rush of the nearby surf, a rhythmic lullaby. The smells of kelp and sea salt were unusually strong—perhaps the tide had receded to reveal a plethora of ocean detritus washed up on the sand. She had a crazy urge to go for a beach walk in her pajamas and slippers. Josh would never have entertained this kind of whim, or maybe he would have, but he might have grumbled all the way.

She silently thanked the cat for bringing her outside at this hour. But how could she long for a night walk, a night swim without Josh? Now she remembered the times his presence had annoyed her, the times she'd wanted to be alone. Once when she'd been reading a particularly suspenseful novel, he'd insisted on talking about an upcoming theater production, and she'd wished he would go away.

Now she longed for him with a heavy ache, as if a block of concrete sat in the pit of her stomach. *I'm sorry I ever wished you were gone. I would give my arms, my legs, my heart to have you back. I'm sorry I want to take a beach walk without you. If you were here, I would want to go with you.*

Her hand was getting cold, holding the plate of tuna. The cat didn't come running toward the smell. Had the poor creature left for a more hospitable house? A rustling sound came from the privet hedge, too small for a cat. Maybe a bird or a squirrel. Lily tiptoed through the grass and left the plate of tuna on the ground close to the hedge. The cat would be able to smell it, and Lily would be able to sleep. But what if the cat were to come back? She couldn't possibly adopt a pet. She could barely keep her own life on track. But she would figure it all out one step at a time.

She went back to bed, realizing only when she got upstairs that her slippers were wet, a few blades of grass stuck to the soles. Josh would've complained and put the slippers in the wash, but instead she left them on the rug, a small luxury. Who cared if a little grass got into the house?

Then she wrapped herself in the covers and lay in the darkness, feeling suddenly small and alone, and she thought maybe it wouldn't be so bad to have a cat sleeping next to her. But no, a cat would have needs. A cat would grow old and die, or maybe it would die before growing old, as Josh had done. And she didn't have time for a pet. She needed to get the local computer guru to set up the retail system for the shop. She needed fixtures. She needed to arrange her vintage displays. Dust the house, pull weeds, write bills—the to-do list went on. She half hoped the tuna would still be there in the morning, an indication that the cat had moved on, but of course, she found the plate empty.

Chapter Four

Kitty

I'm back. How could I leave her alone? I've returned for the promise of more tuna, and also for her unhappy heartbeat. Something is off in the rhythm of blood rushing through her veins. I've listened to heartbeats this sad before, only not on the island. Mostly in the city, where people often live alone in tiny apartments with high windows that could kill me if I were to fall out. Not that I'm afraid of heights.

I trot up to a low bay window of the woman's little yellow cottage. In the overgrown grass, a new sign swings in the wind, indicating a shop, not a restaurant. I can smell restaurants from blocks away. Salmon, grilled chicken, maybe a crab or two. Does she have any food? I can't tell for sure—this shop smells musty and complicated.

I leap onto a rock for a better view inside. Two front rooms are full of clothes. They would make perfect scratching posts in a pinch. Dresses, scarves, hats. Big white statues decked out in colorful, scratchable clothes. Spirits of the lost and lonely have found sanctuary here in the dust and stains and folds. A young woman lingers in a long knit dress, then rises to the ceiling and fades away.

A vague shadow slips along the floor, then up onto a table and expands, taking the barely discernible shape of a man. He's watching the woman, sadness in his empty eyes. He can't see with them, not really, but he senses the woman the way I can sense a mouse hiding beneath a bush.

The woman looks toward him, as if she perceives him, too, but she's staring at a dress on a statue behind him. She reaches right through him, and in touching him, she makes him disappear. Is she aware of these souls that inhabit her shop? Perhaps I need to warn her, but I can't get into the house, can't reach the doorknob, and a doughy woman and skinny man are coming up the sidewalk, stinking of denture cream and the dog they left in the car.

I jump off the rock and move onto the stone path. If only the shop woman would open the door. At times like this, I could use a thumb or two. I stop and pretend to lick my paw, while I secretly assess my situation.

"Oh, look, George, it's a poor little stray!" Just my luck, the doughy woman comes lumbering toward me. Do I look disheveled? I keep my coat groomed.

"You could use a good brushing." She stretches her arms toward me. Arms, so strange, all hairless and dangling. She's the kind of lady who would give me a bath and dress me in doll clothes. I'm not going that route again. But I'm also not the type to dash off at the slightest provocation. No nearby bushes in which to hide, and I can't cross the road with cars rumbling off the ferry.

"Do you think he's hungry?" the doughy woman asks, tiptoeing toward me. "He's probably cold out here with winter coming."

She, thank you very much. How would she like it if I mistook her for a man or even, God forbid, a dog?

George glances at his watch. "Probably belongs to someone, Ida. Let's go."

"Weird eyes!" Ida exclaims, bending down to peer closely at me.

So are yours, all puffy and red.

Ida points at my face. "One eye's green and the other one's blue!"

So what? Ida's about to grab me, so I run up onto the

porch and sit on the prickly welcome mat. I have to pretend I live here.

George wipes his nose with the back of his hand, a crude human gesture. "There you go. This is the cat's house."

I'm closer to the shop now, right at the wooden front door, smelling alcohol, sweat, and soap in the clothes. I hear the sighs and mumblings of phantoms. Something else strange—the shop woman is talking to herself inside, the way crazy people do; but I know she's not crazy, only grieving. Don't ask me how I know. The same way I know when earthquakes are coming or when the spirits won't leave.

Ida won't leave, either. "Maybe he went up on the porch for shelter. It's starting to rain."

George looks at the darkening sky, then at me. "It lives here for sure. We can't have a cat. What about Fifi?"

"She'll get used to having a little brother."

I'll be a dog's sibling when litterboxes freeze over and tuna flies.

"We can't take the cat home," George says with impatience.

"I'm going to see. Wait a minute." She's shuffling up the path. I could run out into the rain, but I hate getting wet. I could hiss at her, but I'm aggressive only when necessary.

Sometimes I almost scare myself, and I don't want to frighten Ida, so I stay put and allow her to pet my head. Then I slink out of reach, jump down off the porch, and slide through a narrow space between the wooden slats.

"Darn! He went in where I can't get him." Ida hesitates a moment, then turns away. She doesn't need me, anyway. She has George and a smelly dog named Fifi. But the shop woman doesn't have anyone except the ghosts that haunt her, and besides, I need shelter from the rain, a warm bed for the night, and at least one decent meal before I sleep.

Chapter Five

This reminder of Josh threw Lily for a loop—a pristine pullover hiding in a box of treasures from a Seattle estate sale. Josh had loved turtlenecks and his favorite color had always been turquoise. If she could banish all shades of blue from the planet, maybe she could forget him for good, but then the world wouldn't have everything beautiful in it— the twilight sky over the Cascade Mountains, the indigo in a double rainbow, the blue-gray waters of the Puget Sound.

But the sweater had to go, even if it was Ralph Lauren

in perfect condition. She couldn't bear to look at it. So she folded the pullover and set it neatly in a box marked *Donations for Families in Need.*

"Why did I bid on this entire collection sight unseen?" she asked the male mannequin by the window. "Now I have to go through all these boxes and—never mind."

When had she started talking to the statue, anyway? It didn't look real, but was only the suggestion of a man— broad shoulders, vague eyes, vague lips. Yet, sometimes she had the strong sensation of being watched, as if Josh's essence had dropped into the mannequin and regarded her through opaque, fiberglass eyes. The prospect should've comforted her, but instead she felt jumpy and spooked.

She turned the statue to face the front window, so he could gaze out across Harborside Road. Josh would've loved the morning mist, the air wafting in fresh from the Pacific Ocean. But he wouldn't have liked the customers traipsing into The Newest Thing across the street, ignoring her boutique. And he wouldn't have liked the noises the cottage made—creaks and groans and strange sighs.

She'd already had a leak repaired in the roof. The contractor had told her the cottage would need a new roof eventually, and maybe she would need a new heating system, too. She'd only been here a month. The rooms felt drafty in spots and too warm in others, as if the house were a planet unto itself, complete with microclimates and self-contained ecosystems swirling inside its walls.

One thing at a time. Right now, forget the house upgrades. I just need to bring in the customers. Why weren't they knocking down the door? She'd installed a painted sign in the yard, on an ornate iron pole that suggested it was a vintage shop. A few curious people had come in, smiling and browsing—stragglers who'd already bought crisp, new outfits at The Newest Thing. What should she expect? She didn't even have a window display, not yet at least. The cottage had stood empty for a long stretch, and it still looked a bit like an abandoned space. She had to give it time—create a pretty tableau in the window, plant flowers in the garden. But would her efforts pay off?

As she rummaged through the last garments in the box, she felt a sudden, sharp panic. What if she failed? What if she ran out of money? What if nobody ever came in? What if The Newest Thing sucked away all her potential customers? She needed to visit the nearby businesses. She'd only been into the Island Creamery. She would go, soon. She would meet her neighbors.

Right now, these dirty shirts needed to be washed with mild, fragrance-free soap. How could people mistreat their clothes, storing cotton in plastic bags? Delicate fabrics needed to breathe, and what was with the toxic mothballs? Herbal southernwood made a much better insect repellent.

She needed a break from the details of laundering, so she got up and stretched, stiff from sitting cross-legged for so long. She headed back to the office for her usual breakfast of grapefruit, toast, and Market Spice tea. The office wasn't another room, really, but rather the dining room closed off from the shop by a standing partition. As always, she perused the *Island Bugle* obituaries—a morbid habit, but she couldn't help herself, and the memorials often celebrated successful lives: a ninety-one-year-old inventor remembered for creating the teleprompter; a ninety-four-year-old Chilean writer known for his "lyrical explorations of eroticism and mortality."

Josh's obituary had read, *Celebrated owner of Vilmont Designs for over a decade, Joshua Vilmont will be remembered for his period costume creations used in theater and film productions far and wide. . . .* She had cried while writing the memorial. *Will be remembered. Will be remembered.* She'd felt as though her fingers bled as she typed, as though her rage would consume her. The universe had cheated her, forcing her to go on living. Somehow she'd believed that if two people were deeply in love, the gods would leave them alone. Josh should've lived to enjoy their golden wedding anniversary. He should've survived long enough to play with their grandchildren.

What was she looking for in these narrow columns of newsprint? To commiserate with others who might understand her pain? She'd written a note to another young widow, *I know exactly how you feel—the disappearing dinner invitations, the looks of pity, the sense of slowly becoming invisible.* She had not heard back.

But she heard from her mother all the time—e-mails, notes, postcards. She also called often, like now, when she should've been at her yoga class. "Are the customers breaking down your door, honey?" Her tinny voice sounded so far away, she could've been talking from the moon instead of California.

Lily gazed out into her empty shop. Well, not empty. Full of the best Chanel, Ralph Lauren, Ferragamo. The clothes were here. The people would come. "Boatloads, Mom. I can't hold off the stampede." She felt a little guilty about lying, but in saying the hopeful words, she could make them come true.

"You're so remote out there."

Lily heard all the things her mother didn't say. *Why did you take off like that? Are you crazy? You can't just uproot yourself. You're losing your mind.* And on a deeper level still: *How could you leave me? Abandon your parents?*

"I don't go to the well for water. I don't use an outhouse. I have electricity—"

"You know what I mean. You're on an island."

"I'm sorry. I didn't mean to be rude, but lots of people live on islands." Lily tightened her grip on the phone. Had she become bitter? She imagined turning into a crotchety old battle-ax of a widow, or however the cliché went. The eccentric woman living alone in her shuttered, dingy house in the boondocks, lashing out at every well-meaning stranger.

"Honey, Dad and I can't help wondering . . ."

Wondering what? Whether she planned to jump off a cliff? Drown herself in the sea? "I'm fine. Don't worry about me."

"I hope you're getting out. Is there anything to do in that small town?"

"Farm festivals. Chocolate tastings. Mammoth fossil hunts. But I don't have time for luxuries. It's a lot of work to set up a shop."

"If you don't go out you might, oh, I don't know. You might get too isolated. Some people end up that way. Or they do drastic things or make decisions they wouldn't otherwise make."

Like move to a sleepy island? Like use all her savings to open a clothing shop in a drafty old cottage? "Moving here *was* getting out." Lily turned the page in the newspaper— another row of obituaries.

"Maybe you could take a buying trip to San Francisco?"

"I've got to get this place off the ground first." Perhaps it would be an impossible task. Lily imagined her parents hopping the next plane, and she would have her social worker mom and high school teacher father offering kind but useless advice about how to run a vintage clothing boutique.

"Dad and I read that fifty percent of all businesses fail in the first year, and ninety-five percent of them fail within five years."

"Thanks for the vote of confidence." Lily focused on the last obituary, for a woman who died of breast cancer at twenty-five. She'd already outlived the woman by several years. She should be grateful for the extra time, for her health, but . . .

"You could move your shop to the city. People are buying used clothes in San Francisco like crazy. Probably in Seattle, too."

"I appreciate the suggestion. I just opened. I have to give it time." Lily closed the newspaper, carefully folded it for the recycling bin.

"If things don't work out, you can always move back home," her mother went on. "The extra room is always here."

A nearly forty-year-old woman living with her parents? Worse things had happened. But it would be a last resort. "Thanks, Mom. Give Dad a hug for me."

She hung up and inhaled the scents of silence, dust, and mothballs. What decision would she have otherwise made? She'd done what was expected of her, at first. She'd attended a widows' support group, but she'd felt light-years removed from the other women, who'd either been much younger or much older than her. She'd fallen into a strange middle zone—not young enough to start fresh, not old enough to share fond memories. So where was she, exactly? In crazy limbo-land, surrounded by old clothes in a quaint but flawed cottage on a remote island where she'd met only a handful of people.

She returned to the front of the shop in time to see a man shuffling up the sidewalk. A paying customer? No, it was Harvey Winslinger, her accountant. She'd hired him the day after she'd arrived on the island, at Jasmine's recommendation. What terrible news did he have to impart?

She rushed to the antique wall mirror to check her hair—wild as usual. And she hadn't dressed well or put on any makeup. Not that she had any interest in Harvey, who was rotund and married, anyway. But she responded the way a reclusive woman responded to any approaching stranger—by becoming self-conscious. She became aware of the dust in the shop, its dimness and mustiness. She looked around at the mess of boxes, the carousels crowded with dresses and shirts, the checkout counter and cash register, the stack of credit card slips still wrapped in plastic, the shelf units that needed to be rearranged, and she suddenly felt overwhelmed. How would she ever organize this place?

As Harvey stepped inside, his face sober, she thought she saw a small shadow dart in after him, but she couldn't be sure.

Chapter Six

Kitty

As I slip in past the rotund man, the spirits seep in around me—through wood and stucco, concrete and glass. Their longing and sadness, hope and worry hover in the dusty air. The woman's former mate is still here, as well—the dark, shapeless ghost of a man who can't let go.

I hide beneath a rack of dresses, belly to the floor, the smells hitting me full force. Smoke and sweat and dead human skin, barely masked by laundry detergent. Mice, insects, a touch of moss. Perfume, tobacco, tears. The bitterness of an orange peel.

I hear a crow landing on the roof, its talons scratching at the shingles; the soft rumble of a furnace, creaks in the walls, and memories of trees inside the floor. Each plank once belonged to a majestic oak, its past imprinted in the wood.

But the sad woman and the rotund man are only dimly unaware of the many layers of reality, of the mingling of the living and the dead. Of what they bring in with them.

From here, I've got a view of the rotund man's black boots and the sad woman's gray running shoes. I have a strong urge to unravel her laces, but I refrain.

"Morning, Lily," the man says in a thick voice, as if he needs to cough up a hairball.

"What are you doing here on a Saturday? Don't you take weekends off?" Lily pretends to straighten a dress. I can tell when people are pretending. They fidget a lot but accomplish nothing. If I had hands, I wouldn't waste them.

"Accountants don't take many holidays in this economy." The man takes off his raincoat and hangs it on a hook by the door. Raindrops are dripping all over the mat, which reminds me: I'm thirsty. I didn't see any good puddles outside.

"I'm sorry," Lily says, although by her tone I can tell she's not sorry at all. People do that—they lie. "It's just— I wasn't expecting you."

"I should've called." He shuffles over, disturbing a sparkly dress on the way, and sets his briefcase on the countertop. He's pigeon-toed, a term people use to describe walking with their feet turned inward. But I think of a pigeon, which reminds me that I'm hungry.

I move over between two gowns, where I get a better view of Lily and the man. He pulls a handkerchief from his pocket, wipes his forehead. "You still don't have any place to sit." He looks around the shop.

"Chairs encourage people to linger," Lily says.

"Isn't that what you want?"

"I want them to buy what they need and leave. I'm not much for trivial conversation."

"Whatever you say." The man snaps open the briefcase and brings out a file folder. Lily peers at what he's showing her—paper with cryptic writing on it—and her right foot taps the floor. I never understood the power of writing to change a person's mood, but I love the smoothness of paper, a perfect surface on which to sit.

"I'm afraid you may need a second loan to meet your expenses," the man says. "I wish I could give you better news—"

"It's all right." Her foot taps faster. Her sad heartbeat quickens. "I'll make do with what I have."

The man clears his throat. "You'll have to work hard

to make a profit." He takes off his glasses, which have steamed up, and wipes them on his sleeve. He looks turtle-like without the spectacles. I've seen a few northwest turtles in the wild, but I've never tried to approach one.

"I haven't even been open a month."

"This is a tough business environment—"

"Thanks, Harvey. I appreciate your help. But I'm confident I can make it work."

So that's what he's called, Harvey. I've never understood the human need for a name. Or two, for that matter.

Harvey's eyebrow twitches. "If it helps at all, my wife enjoys stopping in. She'll tell all her friends."

"Very nice of her."

"But you'll need more than her friends."

"I know. I'm optimistic."

But I sense a current of fear beneath her words.

"Optimism. That's a bonus in this down economy." Harvey leaves the file folder on the counter and closes his briefcase. "Call me if you have any questions." He takes his briefcase and heads to the door. I could leave with him, slink past his legs unnoticed, but the sad woman and the spirits keep me rooted to the spot.

Harvey pulls up his hood as he steps out into the rain.

Lily gazes at the door with a glazed expression, the look people get when they're thinking too hard. She looks up toward the ceiling, as if praying, but I've already seen what it took her much longer to notice. A moth, fluttering! I didn't mean to reveal my presence, but I can't help darting through the shop and jumping onto a table, knocking some ridiculously fragile object to the floor, where it shatters into a rainbow of tiny pieces.

Chapter Seven

Lily

How had this fluffy white cat slipped into the shop? Was this the shadow she'd seen, the slight movement at the corner of her eye? Was it the same cat that had scratched at the front door in the middle of the night? Had the poor thing been lurking near the cottage for days?

For a moment, as the light caught the cat's fur, she thought she saw an aura, a subtle rainbow of color surrounding the cat, as if the creature was not of this world. Most peculiar and ethereal—one lambent eye was blue, the other green. An angel cat.

But when the cat moved into shadow, Lily saw merely a furry animal with dirty paws—a vagrant in search of sanctuary. The cat could be feral, sick, or rabid. And now a precious vintage tea set lay in pieces on the floor—a broken wedding gift from Josh's mother. The jagged shards reflected the sunlight, forming a chaotic mosaic on the floor. *What a grand opening for my boutique. A tea set worth a fortune, destroyed in a heartbeat.* But then, anything beloved could shatter without warning, without hope of repair. Lily knew this only too well.

She had to get rid of the cat, so she propped the front door open. The island air rushed in thicker than usual, like syrup. She waved at the cat, trying to shoo it toward the door. But the cat would have none of it. The stubborn creature jumped onto an antique oak table and batted at a moth. The moth must've been inside the shop the whole time, unless Harvey had brought in the insect as well. Now the moth fluttered upward and landed on the ceiling fixture.

Lily didn't have time for this, not when her shop phone was ringing. Not when she needed to set up a window display, maybe a sidewalk sale, carousels of little black dresses. She wondered what to do. Call Animal Control? Was there even an animal control in this small town? Maybe if she pretended to ignore the cat, it would go away.

But part of her longed for a companion. What if she allowed the cat to stay? Would it keep destroying things? As Lily swept up the pieces of the ruined teapot, the fluffy creature stretched and plopped down on an original Tabriz vintage carpet.

"No, not that one." Lily yanked the rug away and brushed off the fur. The carpet held precious memories. Josh had found the rug, a rare specimen, at a north Berkeley estate sale in California. Now the weave was marred by muddy paw prints.

The cat gazed at Lily then opened its mouth, but only a ragged squeak came out. She had no idea how to pick up an animal without getting bitten or scratched. She'd never had a pet. Her parents had preferred to control their environment, and that meant no unpredictable creatures in the house. But secretly, Lily had always wanted a pet. And here the cat was, looking at her with those softly illuminated eyes. But she couldn't attach herself to anything else living, anything that could die on her.

The moth was in motion again in a frantic whirring of tiny wings, the cat in hot pursuit. As if in a nightmare, Lily raced to catch up, but the cat leaped in an arc, claws splayed out, coming down on Lily's vintage wedding gown, ripping a gash right down the center of the silk bodice.

"No, no! Not the dress!" The mannequin tipped

toward her, but she caught it just in time. "Get out of here, you silly cat!"

"Hello?" a young female voice said behind her. "I heard someone screaming. Were you robbed? Are you okay? I'll call the police!"

Chapter Eight

Kitty

Police? I'm out of here. I've been down that path, the one that
leads to the animal shelter. I'm not going there again. But
somehow I'm trapped in this narrow, dusty space beneath a
monstrous slab of furniture. Wish I could've caught that
moth—

"No need for the police," Lily says. "I wasn't robbed. A
cat ripped my wedding gown. I can't believe this. Classic
Versace."

From here, I can see only the bottom of the girl who
came in—her skinny jeans and red running shoes with

new white laces. She smells of watermelon shampoo and bubble gum, paper and licorice, lip gloss and raspberry perfume. She came from a breakfast of eggs and orange juice, a house of dogs and cats, a sad father who kissed her cheek before he left for the day. Her heart beats with its own kind of loss. But beneath the melancholy lies the resilient brightness of hope, the freshness of youth.

"So you screamed like you were dying," she says. "Just because some little cat ripped an ancient wedding dress?"

I'm not exactly little, per se. I've seen smaller.

"The dress is not ancient," Lily says. "It's vintage." I hear rustling, glimpse her gray sneakers as she walks toward the counter, the wedding gown brushing past me. She's removed the dress from the statue.

"I thought vintage was, like, old wine." The girl's red shoes follow Lily's sneakers.

"Vintage means the best from the past."

This is what I smell in this shop, in the sweat and salty tears. Past joy and pain that humans never wash away. An inky presence, carrying a bitter scent of the afterworld, slides toward Lily and the girl, perhaps attracted by their warmth, their aliveness.

"It's still about old stuff then," the girl says. "So you got married in that dress?"

"A while ago." Lily's shoes come toward me again. She

gets down on her belly and peers at me. "Come on out, kitty." I back up against the wall. From here, I have an exaggerated view of her nose.

"She's scared," the girl says.

Nothing scares me, except certain machines like cars and something called a Vacuum Cleaner.

The girl flops down beside Lily. As she leans forward, her red glasses slip down, and she hastily pushes them up. Now I have a view of two hairless human noses that can't catch a scent to save their lives. Lily and the girl don't seem to notice the inky spirit sliding past them, trying to take on a shape. This troubled being has lingered here a while. And behind the longtime presence, the amorphous aura of Lily's former mate hovers, longing to touch her.

The girl's wavy reddish hair falls over her face. Another whiff of watermelon shampoo. "So where's your husband? Does he work in the city?"

"I don't have a husband anymore." The way Lily speaks, the real story hides beneath her words, like mice hoping not to be found.

"You guys split up?"

"Something like that."

"Bummer." The girl pushes a lock of red hair out of her eyes. "So you're opening up some kind of shop full of old stuff. I mean, vintage."

"I'm trying, but right now I have a problem: the cat. Any ideas?"

The girl sits back beside Lily, the ripped knees of her jeans pointing toward me. "I bet the cat used to live here. Cats can travel thousands of miles to return to their place of origin."

Lily hesitates, as if unsure how to respond. "The previous owner didn't mention—"

"Either way, she's hungry. Give her tuna. Tuna will make her come out, I guarantee it."

"How do you know it's a girl?"

"Just guessing. You can't keep calling her 'it.' "

I slink forward. I'm glad nobody can see me drooling.

Lily gets up. "I think this cat was here once before, and I fed her tuna then, too. I might have another can in the kitchen."

"Do you sleep here, too?" The girl looks around as if she might see a bed stashed nearby.

"I sleep upstairs."

"That's pretty cool. You eat here, sleep here, and you could totally have a shop cat in here."

Shop cat. I like the sound of that—except for the plethora of spirits. They don't all belong in here.

"It's not that I don't want a cat," Lily says slowly. "But I've got a lot of work to do, and I'm not sure I'm ready . . .

Anyway, she must belong to someone. What if we take her to a shelter? Is there a humane society nearby?"

My hackles rise, and a soft rumbling sound rolls in from somewhere. It's me, growling. No way am I going there.

"Not a chance." The girl's face contorts as if she accidentally sucked on a lemon. "Meow City is our only shelter on the island and it's way full."

I'm glad for me but not for my comrades who may have ended up there.

"Then what should I do?" Lily asks.

"If she doesn't belong to a neighbor, then you could talk to my dad. He's the vet up at Island Animal Clinic. I'll call over there."

Vet, animal clinic—not my favorite words. I'll have to escape.

"Can you take her?" Lily says. "I've got things to do."

"The clothes aren't going anywhere. Didn't they belong to dead people?" The girl gets up, her face disappearing from view.

I sense Lily flinching at the words "dead people." "Jennifer Garner wore vintage Valentino to the Oscars. So did Julia Roberts. Reese Witherspoon wore nineteen-fifties Dior."

"Awesome. You know that shop across the street, The

Newest Thing? They don't have any old stuff. Totally different smell in there."

"Oh, what kind of smell?" Lily's voice is dripping acid.

"I dunno—like new and flowery. This place is more like a museum. A messy museum."

"Great, a museum. Um, I'll be right back." Lily hurries into the hall. I can hear her rummaging around, cans clacking in distant cabinets. There are no lingering smells from cooking, so she must subsist on prepared food.

While Lily is gone, the girl's red sneakers move around the shop. I hear papers shifting, clothes coming off hangers. She disappears into the fitting room and returns in high-heeled red shoes and pants with bright green cuffs. When Lily returns, she gasps. "What do you think you're doing? You can't just dress up—"

"Why not? It's fun. You need chairs in here." I hear a clicking sound, like a cell phone camera taking a picture. "How do I look? Totally awesome or what? Do I look like I'm from the olden days?" The girl's high heels tap across the floor.

"Be careful with the hat. The detail is Aurora Borealis rhinestone. Jack McConnell was a premier New York milliner."

"Oh, sorry. I'm putting it back. You know what? I know what a milliner is. Someone who designs hats."

"That's great. Be careful, though. I haven't finished setting up that display—"

"The Newest Thing has an awesome window display.
Did you see?"

"I'm trying not to."

"I want to show you something." The girl's shoes totter
to the counter, more paper rustling. "You circled this.
Estate sale. Everything Must Go. Furniture, silverware,
antiques. No early birds. Up in West Harbor."

"I'm not planning to go. I would have to close the
shop."

"Nobody's even coming in here. You need more lights."

"Oh, is that what I need?"

"Plus, you need a Facebook page, if you don't have one.
I could model the clothes and post the pictures."

"Is that what The Newest Thing does?"

"It's what I would do."

"Is it?" Lily pops open the can of tuna, dumps the fish
onto a plate.

"You need more mirrors. You have only this one."

"One's not enough for you?" Lily puts the plate on the
floor, and I scarf down all the tuna in a couple of bites, not
sure I tasted anything.

"The kitty came out. I told you!" the girl says. "It's like
she hasn't eaten in days."

Not days, exactly. Well, maybe, but so what?

The girl points at me and giggles. "Her tongue is sticking out."

I pull in my tongue. Meant to do that. Sometimes a tongue needs a little air.

Lily glances at me, then sets about moving clothes from one place to another while the girl returns to the dressing room. All the changing that humans do, a waste of time.

I'm sitting on a rug now, spacing out while Lily runs around "tidying up."

When the girl emerges in her street clothes, she plunks me into a box before I can protest. What just happened? "Oh, kitty, quiet down. You'll be okay. What's your name? She needs a name."

"Someone already gave her one, I'm sure," Lily says.

I did have a name, but I can't remember, and it doesn't matter now.

"But you have to give her one. We all have names. You have a name, don't you?"

"Lily. And you?"

"Bish. It's not short for anything. Just Bish. You could call her Cottonpuff or Snowball or . . . What's white? Dandruff?"

"I don't want to name the cat."

"Snowflake then."

"She's more of a Blanche. Kind of crazy. But forget it—"

"Blanche, I like that!" Bish says.

"It's from *A Streetcar Named Desire*."

"A streetcar named what?"

Someone's taping the box, poking airholes. I'm in a fix, but I'll make it through this—I've experienced worse. I sense Lily's worry swirling through the air, and through a peephole, I see her frowning out the window toward the shop across the street, her eyes full of doubt.

Chapter Nine

Lily

Lily carried the box, with the cat inside, across the street to The Newest Thing, a storybook boutique in a rectangular redbrick building. Whimsical wind chimes hung from the eaves, and the latest fashions and handbags were carefully arranged in the large bay window. She felt some trepidation about going inside, but she had tried the Island Creamery and the Apothecary Shop, but they had not claimed the cat.

Now here she was, inside a rival dress shop that breathed freshness and light. Bish had been right. Everything smelled new. The owner had taken care to arrange the clothes in beautiful, well-lit configurations. Lily spotted six customers browsing the carousels of silk and chiffon, wool and rayon, not counting the women in the fitting rooms.

She had an urge to run back to the cottage, pack up all her things, and leave. Why even bother? She could never compete. She would never be able to wash out the smells of dust and smoke and sweat from the wrinkled old garments in her shop.

But she reminded herself that the clothes weren't "old," they were classics. Each one told its own story.

Still, how could she transform the messy rooms into anything to match this beauty? Josh had always been the interior decorator with the aesthetic eye. Lily had been the one to choose quirky clothes on impulse, to learn the history of each piece, to make adjustments, to keep the books, to keep Vilmont Designs in the black. But now she had no real idea how to attract buyers.

Behind the counter, a young woman, trim and close-cropped in every way, sat on a stool with her head bent over a smartphone, her thumbs tapping away, texting someone. The soft rustle of fabrics blended with pop music emanating from a hidden stereo system, but she didn't seem to notice the world around her, including her customers.

The cat remained quiet as Lily wound her way to the

counter, sidestepping displays and taking note of the artful layout, the cabinet of imported French soaps. The woman looked up only when Lily was standing right in front of her. "Can I help you?" Her eyes flickered with annoyance. Her name tag read "Chris."

"I wonder if you know anything about this cat," Lily began in a low voice, and then quickly told her story.

Chris shrugged, frowning slightly at the box, as if it were a burr that Lily had carried inside on her coat. "I don't know. Don't have a clue. I don't think Florence has any cats. She would have a fit if anyone brought a cat in here. She's the owner, not me."

Not me. So this Florence could afford to hire at least one employee. She'd probably been in business a while. Lily could see that her clothes were overpriced. "Is she here? I'd like to ask her directly."

"Oh, hell no. Flo's hardly ever here." Chris laughed softly. Her silver hoop earrings and small silver nose ring glinted in the light.

Hardly ever here, and yet her shop thrived. Or did it? A woman headed for the door empty-handed, and Chris watched with a standard brand of indifference. Did she not have an investment in the shop's success?

"Could you call Flo?" Lily said. "Just in case. I would hate to take the cat to the shelter and then find out—"

"She doesn't have a cat," Chris said, her face becoming closed and guarded. "I would know. I work here, like, five days a week."

Five days a week? What did Flo do all that time? Did she have another shop? "Could the cat belong to someone else around here? I'm pretty new in town. Maybe you have an idea?"

"Nobody has a cat like that." Chris made as if to return to her texting, when a chunky woman, with a mountain of permed white hair, came up and draped a flowing pink shirt across the counter. "I love this but do I have to dry clean it? It says dry clean only. What alternative do I have to all those chemicals?"

Chris read the label inside the collar. "It says dry clean only."

"I realize that. It's a beautiful shirt, but—"

"Dry clean only. I would follow the directions."

"You can use a mild detergent and hand wash," Lily said. "Dry cleaning chemicals can be harsh—"

"That's what I think!" The woman looked at Lily and smiled. "For this shirt, though?"

"You want to protect the shape of the fabric, so use cold water and don't wring or twist."

"How do you know all this?"

The cat mewled pitifully, and Lily's arms were beginning to hurt from holding the box. "I have some experience with rayon. I just opened my shop across the street, Past Perfect. Vintage clothing."

"Rayon is vintage?" The woman glanced out the window.

"Sometimes, yes."

"Well, I'll be. You're in the old Candy Cottage? I've got to stop in there."

Chris frowned. "You can't return the shirt after you wash it, if you're not following directions."

Lily touched the shirt. It looked like rayon, felt like rayon, and the label—yes, it read "rayon." She had learned to identify the textures of various fabrics. "In my shop, you can return a shirt like this even if you've washed it. I guarantee my clothes have already been washed anyway, some of them multiple times. Vintage fabrics are hardier than today's fragile—"

"Do you want the shirt or not?" Chris cut in, tapping the counter.

The woman hesitated, then sighed and dug into her purse. "I do love the rose print on the front." She smiled at Lily again. "Thanks, dear, for all your help. You are . . . ?"

"Lily Byrne. I would give you a business card, but I don't have any yet."

"That's okay. I'll stop in."

Chris pursed her lips as she rang up the shirt, and Lily hurried out into the cool, spitting rain. She'd just helped a rival shop make a sale, when the owner wasn't even there and her employee couldn't care less about the business. And all that Lily got in return was a homeless, mewling cat in a box and her own messy, empty shop. But still, her spirits rose a little. She had an advantage—something that just might make a difference. She genuinely loved the clothing in her shop. She and Josh had chosen each piece. She wouldn't hire someone like Chris, even if she could afford an employee. She would stay in her boutique to answer questions in person, to impart her knowledge of fabrics and how to care for them, if only the customers would come inside.

Chapter Ten

Kitty

We're in a car, and cars never lead anywhere good. The drone of the engine sears my eardrums, and the stink of exhaust nauseates me. Through holes in the box, I can see Lily staring ahead with glazed eyes. I get mesmerized sometimes, too—by clouds or birds, but never by windshield wipers.

"I shouldn't be driving you. Josh would be the one doing this . . ."

The shapeless spirit? I didn't know ghosts could drive. He's not here, anyway. Through another airhole in the box,

I see Lily's white-knuckled fingers gripping the steering wheel. I've held on that tightly before with my claws, when I was up a tree. I meant to be there. I was merely taking precautions.

"Oh, come on. It's not that bad. You're turning me into an emotional wreck. Can't you quiet down?"

I suppose I'm making noise. But who wouldn't, in my situation? How would she like to be stuck in a box in a roaring killing machine?

"He once picked up a dead chickadee from the condo balcony. It hit the window and broke its neck. Why do birds do that? Fly to their doom?"

Who cares why? A dead bird is a dead bird and a tasty one if it's fresh.

"Made me sad to see that little thing lying there. When I called the Audubon Society for advice, a volunteer suggested keeping the windows dirty so birds wouldn't see their reflections. So I haven't washed the cottage windows yet, but I should, if I want to compete with The Newest Thing. The windows are clean there, clean and shiny."

People often do this, talk to themselves under the pretense of talking to me.

"Josh would've probably kept you, but he was allergic. He said, 'If our kid wants a pet, I'll try those allergy injections.' But did he want a girl or a boy? Or both? We never had a chance to talk about it. Not that we could've chosen. We didn't even get to say good-bye."

So her mate departed in a sudden way. No wonder she talks to herself. No wonder he hangs around. Perhaps he doesn't even realize he's dead.

Now she's pulling out a loose collar from beneath her shirt—or what humans call a "necklace." She touches a ring that hangs from the necklace. The gold metal glints in the light. Something else, too—a tiny glass vial. I know what's inside. Human ashes give off a dull odor, different from wood ash and barely detectable, which is probably why I didn't smell them before.

She tucks the necklace back under her shirt, and I sense the clinic ahead. I shudder as she parks the car beneath a fir tree. "What if I leave you on the porch with a note? Okay, quiet down. I was only thinking aloud."

I wish she would do less of that. My voice is going hoarse as she carries me inside, still in the box. Then all sounds disappear from me. We're in hell—a crowded waiting room that reeks of dog and disinfectant. A tall man holds a trembling, yapping poodle in his lap; a woman sits next to a giant golden retriever, its tongue hanging out; a tiny man holds a cat carrier in his lap. I smell a depressed black tomcat with a damaged leg.

Lily props the box on the countertop. Through the

pathetic airholes, I glimpse the girl at the desk. She looks up at us and smiles. "You're Lily, and this is the kitty you found."

The girl speaks with a slight accent. No wrinkles, but her eyes look old. Pulled back into a tight ponytail, each strand of hair is exactly the same shade of solid yellow.

"Your earrings are vintage," Lily says.

The girl touches her right ear. "They're begonias. My sister found them at a garage sale for two dollars."

"They're worth about fifty."

"Then she got a good deal!"

"She did." Lily glances at her watch. "So I'll leave the cat with you?"

"You have to see the doctor."

"But—"

"Please fill this out." As the girl stands to hand Lily a clipboard, I glimpse her large belly. She's about to pop a litter; actually, only one.

Lily's face has gone pale, a strange look in her eyes—the look that people get when they're either wishing for something or regretting some decision. "I don't have time to fill out a form—"

"Just do the best you can."

Lily sighs and looks at the girl's name tag. "I'll try. Thank you, Vanya." She turns away, puts me on a chair, and sits next to me. She stares at the paper on the clip-board, screwing up her eyebrows. "I don't know your age, sex, or medical history. How am I supposed to answer all these questions?"

She jots a few cryptic notes, then gets up and returns the form, and Vanya slips the page into a file folder and leads us down the hall and into a small room. "Dr. Cole will be with you soon. Make yourself at home."

She waddles out and shuts the door.

"Make myself at home?" Lily says, rubbing her arms. "I can barely breathe in here."

Likewise. She goes on babbling while I press my eye to the biggest hole and take in my surroundings. To fight a successful battle, one must know the enemy. Jars of cotton balls and spray bottles are lined up on a narrow counter-top next to the sink. The tub of treats is designed to fool unsuspecting victims. A dog might fall for that one, but not me. Worse, a morbid drawing of a cat hangs on the wall, the skin cut away, showing a side view with labeled arrows pointing to various internal organs. I'm shivering all over, not liking the smells in here.

Footsteps approach in the hall and the doctor bursts in frowning, like a storm cloud, his dark hair mussed. His white lab coat flaps over faded blue jeans. He washed up but he can't mask the traces of blood and sickness, all mixed in with soap and sweat and the scrambled eggs he ate for breakfast. He looks nothing like his offspring, Bish. She has a delicate nose and fragile skin sprinkled with freckles. She has not inherited his blocky features or square jaw.

And she has not inherited his terrible discontent, his slow heartbeat full of bitterness. His loss is not like Lily's, not full of wistfulness and happy memories. No, his heart is brooding, angry, and trapped, and he doesn't see any way out of the darkness.

Chapter Eleven

The doctor took so long, Lily thought she might grow old and die while she waited, shriveling to dust before he even arrived. She pictured her shop sitting empty and dark, the sign swinging in the wind, customers pressing their noses to the window, then walking away.

How many opportunities had she missed in the last hour? Maybe only a few, but the point was, she wasn't in her boutique. She was here in a stinky, noisy animal clinic in a room as small as a closet, trying to ignore the dank smell of wet dog and the distant mewling of distressed cats.

Now the vet breezed inside, his head bent over the cat's open file folder. No apology, no acknowledgment of Lily's presence. When he finally glanced up at her, she thought he looked vaguely familiar. She'd seen him in Jasmine's Bookstore, only he'd looked relaxed. Now he was all business in a white lab coat, and if he recognized her from their brief encounter, he showed no sign. He looked distracted, disheveled, and full of his own self-importance.

"Ben Cole," he said in a gruff voice, almost like a bark. Perhaps he spent too much time around dogs. He reached out to shake her hand. She bristled, giving his fingers only a perfunctory squeeze. His hand felt warm, solid, and damp. Stubble formed a shadow on his jaw, and his eyes were pale gray, nearly colorless. His nose had a slight bump, as if someone had punched him a long time ago. Not surprising, she thought, considering his utter lack of regard for his clients' time.

"Lily Byrne." She pulled back her hand and wiped off the dampness on her jeans. His gaze lingered on her face, and then he bent and peered into the box. The cat let out a tiny meow. He straightened, frowning. "You need a carrier, not a cardboard box."

Now he was giving her advice? "The box worked fine.

The cat doesn't belong to me. Bish said you might take her."

"She told you that? If I had to take in every animal—"

"But I can't keep this cat."

He said nothing, but at least he didn't press her for a reason. What would she tell him? That she feared the cat would ruin her shop? She couldn't take care of another fragile living creature. She felt fragile enough already.

The room seemed to shrink around her, her pulse pounding in her ears. The hospital sounds faded into a faraway hum as the doctor reached into the box and expertly picked up the cat. Lily felt inept as she watched him arrange the kitty on his lap and examine her. She purred and squinted up at him, and he squinted back. Was this some form of secret feline communication?

This is his job. He's supposed to be good at it, Lily thought, but she wondered what she herself was truly good at. She'd managed to keep Josh's design business running from the back office, but adding up columns of numbers had not prepared her for this solitary life, her own shop, or the possibility of failure. Now there was this cat, a small creature but to Lily, a huge intrusion. Was this what it meant to grieve? Was it normal for every small thing to feel immense?

What would she say to this vet if he were to walk into

her shop, looking for something to wear? Would she point him to a Ralph Lauren turtleneck or a flannel plaid shirt? Or would she be tongue-tied?

As she watched him work, so calm and sure, she wanted his boldness, his confidence, maybe even a little of his inflated ego.

"She's an odd-eyed cat," he said. "It's a feline form of complete heterochromia."

"Hetero-what?"

"Lack of pigment in one eye. In this case, in her green eye. Some white cats are deaf as well, but she has a sharp sense of hearing. She's been out there a while, but she's calm and pretty tame."

"Calm? She wasn't like this in my shop. She was running all over the place, chasing a moth. She damaged my wedding dress." She hadn't meant to say that last part about the dress. She didn't want to reveal anything about herself, but now she felt as if her entire history was written on her face.

He looked at her. "Cats bring us down to earth, force us to reevaluate our priorities."

She had no idea how to respond. He knew nothing about her except that she owned a clothing store and a damaged wedding dress. Who was he to judge her? "My priorities are just fine, thank you. Can we hurry this up? I need to get back."

He opened the cat's mouth and checked her teeth. "She's older than she looks. Maybe nine, maybe ten. She's a senior cat."

"A senior, great." The poor thing could die at any moment, and didn't old cats have all kinds of health issues?

"She grooms herself well but long-haired cats need extra help. They need regular brushing."

"Tell that to her owner." Lily knew she sounded rude, but the doctor's attitude chafed her. She hadn't anticipated a full medical workup for the cat. She hadn't planned to be here at all. She had no time to brush an animal. She could barely remember to brush her own hair.

He put the cat on the floor and allowed her to explore. "She may not have an owner. She may be a stray."

"Either way, she's not mine. Can we do only the basics? How much will all this cost? I mean, this is the last thing I expected—"

"We'll do our best to accommodate your financial constraints."

Her face flushed. *Financial constraints?* Who did he think he was? She imagined picking up the glass jar of pet treats and whacking him over the head. "I have no financial constraints," she said, a lie. "But her owners will have to reimburse me. They're probably looking all over for her. If you can't keep her, I guess I have to take her to the shelter."

His expression didn't change, but a muscle twitched in his jaw. He jotted something in the chart. "It's your decision. However, you could keep her for now and post flyers. If she's lost, and someone tries to claim her, they should be able to identify her."

"I wish I could do more for her, but I've got a lot on my plate. I'll pay to get her brushed and cleaned up, and then I'll take her to the shelter."

"Fine. Suit yourself. I'll be a few minutes." He scooped up the cat and went out into the hall without looking back. The door slammed behind him. So this was a good plan. The basics and no more, and then she would be done with the cat.

Chapter Twelve

Kitty

On the drive back to the shop, we stopped in at Meow City, where I cringed in the carrier until Lily hurried me back out to the car. She couldn't bear to abandon me among the imprisoned. It took the entire journey, with a stop at the pet supply store, for the alarming smells and sounds to fade from my mind.

Back in the cottage, the spirits have concentrated into a dense mass. A young woman, who died in a violent accident, clings to a floral dress that belonged to her daughter. How can she know that her child long ago passed into the next realm?

Lily shivers a little. She turns up the thermostat, then tries to confine me to the kitchen, but my voice and my claws scratching at the door prove too much for her.

"This situation is temporary," she says as she opens the kitchen door again. I run out into the hall. The spirit of her former mate slides along next to her shadow, occasionally blending into the darkness and then slipping away. Another spirit hides out of sight, the one that has lingered here for eons. Lily stops and looks around, her brows furrowed, then rubs her arms and shivers again.

"Cold pockets," she says to me. "Maybe the place is haunted. Wouldn't that be my luck? And what am I going to do with you?"

I sit on a threadbare rug and watch her while she calls one shelter, then another, and then another one farther away—trying to find a way to get rid of me.

"Everyone's full. Unbelievable. Oh, stop staring at me that way, as if I'm betraying you. How am I going to get anything done when I have to watch you?"

I turn away and trot up to sit in the empty front window. Fascinating, the commotion in the shop across the street. After a while, Lily drags a statue, clad in a soft orange dress, toward the window and props it on the wide ledge next to me. She places a pair of glittery shoes and a handbag next to the statue, then arranges another plastic woman on the ledge, this one wearing a shiny blue gown.

"Who can resist vintage silk?" she says, grinning. "I can do this, can't I, kitty?"

I lick my paw.

She peers outside and frowns. "What are they doing over there? How did they come up with that? A mannequin lying on her side in a winter coat? The Newest Thing, my foot." She looks at her own display. "Maybe I need a winter scene, too. How do I find a mannequin that can lie on its side that way? But this is what people are dreaming of, right? A summer night on the town?"

Someone is shuffling up the sidewalk, stopping to peer in at me. Oh no, it's Ida. She's coming this way. I run to hide beneath a rack of black dresses.

"Could this be a customer?" Lily says, her eyes lighting up. "There, you see? My display is already working."

Horror of horrors, Ida shuffles in, without George this time, but I catch a disgusting whiff of Fifi.

"So this is where the white kitty lives!" Ida exclaims. "I saw him in the window."

"Actually, she's a girl," Lily says. "She just showed up. Is she yours?"

"I wish she was. She's beautiful. I can't believe I never stopped in here."

"I just opened," Lily says, hurrying after Ida, who is browsing now, touching this and that.

"You're a little off the beaten path." Ida looks across the street at the comings and goings in the other shop. Then she smiles at Lily. "But now that I'm here, I'll look around."

"Please do."

Please don't.

"I'm in a buying state of mind. What can you show me?"

I'm going to have to stay hidden, as Ida might be here for a while.

Chapter Thirteen

Lily

Lily looked around at her messy shop, bewildered. This doughy woman hadn't been drawn by the window display. She'd come to see the cat. Some deep need emanated from her, a desire that had long lain dormant. If she were to walk into The Newest Thing, what would happen? Chris would look up and nod at her, then return to her smartphone. Or maybe she wouldn't look up at all. Ida would browse in complete anonymity. But here in Past Perfect, Lily could step in to help. She could make a difference. But how?

"I've got some lovely dresses," she said. Her voice came out rusty. She cleared her throat. "If you're looking for a dress, that is. Are you?" Oh, she sounded ridiculous. If only she could erase her words and start again.

The doughy woman tapped her chin with a chubby forefinger, in which a gold ring was deeply embedded. "Maybe a dress. I was supposed to come here for something. The kitty called to me, not in words, but you know . . ." She glanced down at her jeans, the shapeless kind with an elastic waist; and at her sensible, rubber-soled shoes. She wore an oversized, baggy polyester shirt beneath her sagging jacket. It was as if she were looking at someone else, some body that she could not recognize as hers.

What would Josh have done? What could Lily do? She could make a personal connection, so she reached out and shook the woman's cool, soft hand. "I'm Lily. Maybe if you tell me more about what you're looking for, I can help you."

"I'm Ida," the woman said, withdrawing her hand, "and I'm looking for, oh, I don't know. Something pretty and unique."

The cat tiptoed over and rubbed against Lily's legs, and in that instant, she heard the words that Ida didn't say. *I'm looking for happiness. I'm looking to stop time. I'm looking not to get any older or fatter than I already am. I'm looking for my husband to look at me the way he used to. I'm looking for the impossible.*

Across the street, The Newest Thing's window scene had grown more elaborate, with snow and ski poles and a sprinkling of flakes on the mannequin's coat. A new neon sign winked on above the door. Ida glanced across the street, her eyes bright. "Maybe I should just . . ." she began.

"Just?" Lily followed Ida's gaze. A young woman came out of The Newest Thing carrying a large shopping bag. She glanced across the street at the mannequins in Lily's window, looked right and left, then crossed the street at an angle toward the Island Creamery.

Lily looked over at the cat, who sat in an elongated, rectangular sun spot near a shelf of silk scarves. If the cat had been visible in the window, would the girl have braved coming over? Maybe Lily should've bought a cottage closer to the curb, without a garden to traverse between the sidewalk and the porch. It was almost as if some invisible barrier prevented people from coming up to the door—unless, possibly, they saw the cat.

But the cat wasn't going to stay. The shop would have to speak for itself. Lily would have to help Ida on her own. *Something pretty and unique. A shape. Hope. The impossible.*

"I have an idea for you." Lily brought out a yellow and

black chiffon dress that tapered in at the waist. "I'm not sure about the size, but I have a feeling it will highlight your beauty."

Ida's face lit up. "Beauty?" She seemed to hold on to the word as if it were a life jacket keeping her afloat.

"Yes, um . . ." Lily looked over at the cat, who was busy grooming her face. Her fur shone silver in the pale autumn sunlight. "The cat pointed this one out."

Ida's eyes widened. She glanced at the cat, then whispered to Lily, "The kitty talks to you? I knew it."

"Well, she doesn't talk, exactly, but we communicate by . . . squinting. Yes, squinting. The cat squints at a dress—"

"And you have to pick it!"

Lily nodded, feeling foolish for lying. "This is a silk chiffon sunshine dress from the fifties. Grecian style with the pleated bodice. The back zipper was probably added later."

Ida flipped the dress over. "How interesting about the zipper. So the cat thought this would make me beautiful?"

"Highlight the beauty already inside you." *There, that sounded better.* "Each piece is one of a kind, so I don't have other sizes."

"I'm not worried." Ida winked at the cat, as if the two shared a secret, then lumbered toward the fitting room.

When she finally came out, the dress had transformed her in an indefinable way.

"Heavenly," Ida said, standing stiffly in front of the mirror. She had begun to take shape. She curved in at the waist. She had discernible cleavage. Her ankles showed. They were surprisingly thin.

She sucked in her belly, puffed out her chest. "You can fix the waist, can't you?"

Such a thing could be done, but the dress needed more fabric. "That kind of silk is hard to find these days."

"Can't you order it in?"

"It would be difficult. Dress fabrics aren't like shades of paint that you can mix. The colors won't match up."

Ida rested her hands on her hips, then let out a long breath. "Ah, well, maybe I could buy the dress as is. I'll lose weight. I'll go on another diet, but not that Atkins one this time."

Lily knew diets rarely worked. What needed to change was one's lifestyle. Grief could work wonders, for example, to help a woman grow thin. "It's entirely up to you," she said.

"Let me think about it." As Ida went back to change, Lily wondered if she should have tried harder to make the dress fit. Could she have offered alterations, but what would she have done about matching the fabric?

Ida stayed in the dressing room so long, Lily began to worry. Finally the door squeaked open, and Ida shuffled out, still in the dress, her face red. "I'm afraid I can't, um, get this thing off. The zipper is stuck."

"Turn around. Let me try." Lily pulled at the zipper, but the dress seemed fused to Ida's body. "No dice, I'm afraid."

Ida's chin trembled. "Try again."

Lily tried again and again, without success. A cool breeze wafted over her, although the door was shut. The hair rose on her arms. "We'll figure this out," she said, stepping back. "Maybe try pulling the dress up over your head?"

"I tried that. It's stuck on my hips."

Lily had been certain the dress would fit. She tried the zipper several more times. Ida tried pulling off the dress to no avail.

"There's one thing we can do, but it's a bit radical," Lily said finally. The cat sat upright, nose to the air. Her ears twitched as she looked around, then she shot an upward glance at nothing.

"What do you have in mind?" Ida said, her eyes pleading.

"Stay here." Lily headed back to the office, her heart pounding, and rummaged in her desk drawers. She grabbed a pair of fabric scissors and returned to the shop. "I'm so sorry, but I can't see an alternative. I'm not sure how to go about doing this, but I'm going to try to cut this dress right off you."

Chapter Fourteen

Kitty

"That went well," Lily says as we watch Ida hurry off down the path. "She'll never come in here again. Everyone in town will hear about how I had to cut the dress off her, and my shop will be closed in no time." Her eyes brighten with tears.

What can I tell her? That an unhappy spirit may have been responsible for this small disaster? As Ida hummed in the dressing room, an inky presence, the one that has been here a long time, seeped under the door and cast its spell on her. When she came out, the dress was too tight. The dark spirit lingered, then slipped away into the ether.

Now the other ghosts grow restless in the gray evening as Lily rearranges her shop. "I really tried to help Ida in a way that she could never be helped in The Newest Thing. You know, kitty? Now all I've got are scraps of cloth on the alterations table. No more chiffon dress. But I'm not giving up."

Fine with me.

She carries piles of clothes from one place to another, hangs up dresses, adjusts the statues in the window. I'm content to sit on a pile of men's neckties, absorbing the layers of life and death shifting through the room.

Finally, Lily goes off to bed, and when the house is quiet and dark, my world comes alive. My legs begin to itch. I tear around, my claws scrabbling on the hardwood floor. I bat at dust motes and leap at moths flitting outside beneath the porch lights.

"Kitty! What are you doing?" Lily is up now, coming after me. She's nearly tripping over the cuffs of her pajamas. Interesting hairdo, as well. "I can't believe you woke me up at this hour."

I tumble down the stairs and veer into her office, jump onto the desk, and knock some paper onto the floor.

"Are you crazy? What's wrong with you?" She follows me into the kitchen. She flips on the light, and I squint in the sudden brightness. A ball of dust requires my attention—

"Kitty, no! Don't eat that." Lily is bending down to pull the dust from my mouth. She throws the clump in the garbage. Then she sits in the breakfast nook, head in her hands.

My insides feel funny; oh no.

"Are you throwing up? Oh, kitty!"

Can't help it, I'm heaving, but I feel better now.

"I can't believe this is happening." She's flipping open her cell phone, pressing buttons. "Oh, Dr. Cole. I'm so sorry I woke you. I thought I would get the emergency . . . This is Lily Byrne. It's the cat. She threw up. What should I do?"

I'm hiding under the table.

Lily is listening, then she says, "Tomorrow? But I'm afraid she's ill, and I can't have anything else die on me."

I can almost feel his surprise. I'm a bit surprised, too. He says something, and then Lily says, "You're coming here? I'm on Harborside Road. I'm sorry, I know—thank you."

She hangs up and bends to pet me. "Don't throw up again, please." In her eyes, I see the reflection of my face staring back at me, my elegant whiskers, tufted ears. I also see the depth of her worry. I feel her soul softening, her face close to mine. I can't help lifting my chin and then just barely, I touch my nose to hers.

Chapter Fifteen

When had Lily last entertained a guest? Before Josh's death, and never so late at night. She barely had time to put on a robe and slippers, brush her hair, and wipe up the vomit before she heard a knock on the back door. How had Dr. Cole arrived so quickly?

The cat ran to the door, but when Lily opened it, the poor thing took one look at the vet and dashed away.

"She wasn't scared of you at the clinic," Lily said, shaking her head. "Maybe she senses something different."

Dr. Cole stood on the porch, unsmiling, a black veterinary bag in hand. He looked almost human in an open windbreaker, blue sweater, jeans, and hiking boots—the way he'd looked in the bookstore. Except for the scowl.

Lily stepped back and ushered him inside. "Did you have trouble getting here?"

"Took a wrong turn in Seattle, ended up in Portland, but eventually I found my way."

Was this his brand of humor? "You must've driven at the speed of sound."

"Or light." He took in her robe and slippers, a slightly irritated look on his face. Should she have donned an evening dress?

"Come on in. I appreciate you driving here in the middle of the night." She pulled the robe closed. She hoped the necklace didn't show. She didn't want to have to explain about the ring and the vial.

He wiped his hiking boots on the mat, then stepped past her, closing the door behind him. He looked toward the kitchen. "Where did she go?"

"She must be hiding. Do you think she might've eaten something bad?"

"I have to see her first. You could've put her in the carrier."

"I didn't realize she would run from you." Was there no other veterinarian in this town? Someone more like James Herriot?

His frown deepened, bushy eyebrows brooding and almost Neanderthal. "Did you leave anything lying around? Rubber bands? Jewelry? Buttons?"

"I don't leave things lying around."

Dr. Grinch followed her into the kitchen. "You have to treat a cat like a toddler. She may put things in her mouth. Floss, thread."

She didn't need a lecture. "I've never had a toddler, and she didn't get into anything."

"Did you feed her anything different?"

"I gave her only cat food."

"I see." He did not look convinced.

"Can I take your jacket?" Why did she bother with politeness?

"I'll keep it on. Where did she go?"

"Probably upstairs. This way." She turned and led him through the kitchen, imagining Bish and her mother waiting at home, disturbed by his late-night foray into downtown Fairport. Or were they glad to be rid of him?

He followed her up the stairs, his boots clopping on the steps. He should've taken them off, but she did not want to be rude and point this out.

In her room, he glanced at the bed, the vintage dressing table, the set of shelves lined with books arranged by height. She hadn't yet unpacked a few boxes. She realized now that her bedroom screamed "widow," from the dusty, unused bottle of Dior perfume on the dressing table, to the cotton bra thrown over the back of a vintage chair. If she was going to show the bra to a visitor, she thought, at least she could've chosen a Victoria's Secret black lace number, but she no longer even owned such a thing.

Dr. Cole glanced at the bra, and his face flushed. Lily ran over, grabbed the bra, and stuffed it into a drawer. Her cheeks heated again. "Sorry. I wasn't expecting anyone."

"I'm the one intruding." He glanced at the book of poems on the bedside table. "I have that one in paperback."

"You have a book of poems?" She could barely contain her surprise.

"Picked it up a while ago."

"You're into poetry. I mean, that's great." She tried to imagine him reading poetry, but no image came to her.

"When I get time to read."

"I've only read a couple of the poems. Jasmine gave me the book."

He nodded, brows raised. "Ah, I saw you in the bookstore."

"And I saw you."

"And now here we are."

"Here we are." She became aware of the permeable membrane between her interior life and the world outside. If Dr. Cole happened to open the top drawer of the bureau, he would find Josh's briefs, undershirts, and socks still folded inside. He would think her foolish and sentimental, or maybe just plain weird. She'd kept a few of Josh's jackets, too, and a few pairs of shoes, all hidden in the closet.

Dr. Cole's gaze rested on a twitching tail sticking out from under the bed. He put his bag on the dresser, got down on his knees, and peered at the cat. Then he pulled her out and tried to examine her, but she wriggled away and slid back under the bed.

He stood and brushed off his jeans. "She seems all right, but I suggest we give her time to calm down. Then I'll take another look."

"I'm relieved that she *seems* okay, at least." Lily had a strange urge to push him into the hall. She'd become protective of her space. She'd kept Josh close to her, and now Dr. Cole's imposing presence was getting in the way. He was alive, breathing, solid, and no matter how unlikable he was, he was a man. She felt fascinated by him, by his complex broodiness, and yet she felt guilty for even wondering anything about him, as if she were betraying Josh.

Dr. Cole stepped into the hall, and she turned off the

bedroom light. For a moment, the two of them fell into the strange intimacy of darkness.

"Would you like a drink while we wait for the kitty to come out?" What was she saying? Did she even have a drink to offer him?

"I could use a cup of coffee."

At three a.m.? "Coffee, of course." Had she unpacked the coffeemaker?

He stepped back into the bedroom, brushing past her, and grabbed his veterinary bag. Then he followed her down into the kitchen again and stood at the counter while she rummaged around in the cabinets. His presence made the room seem smaller and somehow bare. She should have fruits and vegetables on the countertop, onions hanging in a basket, but cooking hadn't interested her much lately.

"What did you mean?" he asked.

"About what?" Why couldn't she find any coffee?

"About not wanting to have anything else die on you?"

"Oh." She froze, her hand on a packet of teabags. "My husband. He passed away several months ago."

"I'm sorry."

"It's all right."

"I understand why you called about the cat."

"Maybe I was silly."

"No, not at all." He didn't ask any more questions.

An awkward silence.

"So, how is Bish?" she asked, still rummaging.

"She says you're taking her to some estate sale."

"Oh, I'm not going."

"She seems to think you are."

"I'm pretty sure I told her I'm not." She couldn't find any coffee. Since when had she become such a hermit, with nothing to offer a visitor? "I'm afraid I've only got Ovaltine and Earl Grey tea. Herbal teas, too."

"Ovaltine? Who drinks Ovaltine anymore?"

"It's left over from . . . before." From Josh.

"Quik tasted better than Ovaltine."

"I remember Quik. Strawberry Quik was my favorite. All that sugar, with a picture of a pink rabbit on the label."

He looked out the window at shadows in the moonlit backyard. "The name got corrupted. Strawberry Quik is now a code word for a kind of crystal meth."

"How do you know that?"

"Read it online."

It was so strange to have him in here, someone so different from Josh. Dr. Cole was unreadable, while Josh had worn his emotions on the outside. He'd loved clothes but had not been much interested in using a computer.

"I'd offer you the real Quik if I had it, but it's the Ovaltine or tea."

"A glass of water will be fine." He stood so still compared to Josh, who'd always been doing something with his hands.

She poured a glass of water. "Sorry about the coffee."

"I can do without." He pointed out the window, looking upward. "That's an old maple."

"Came with the property."

"My wife used to press maple leaves into books."

Lily wondered about his wife who, she thought, must be delicate and exuberant like Bish. "I used to do things like that. But I pressed flowers, too."

He nodded, swigged down the water, and put the glass on the counter. "Where is the vomit?"

"Excuse me?" She blinked at him, then remembered. "Oh." She pulled out the garbage can from beneath the sink. "Are you sure you want to see it? It's gross."

"I'm used to gross." He opened his bag, extracted a pair of vinyl surgical gloves, and started picking through the garbage. Now he truly knew how Lily lived—on microwaveable meals, prepared breakfast cereals. Tea bags. Garbage could reveal too much about a person's life or lack thereof.

"There, in that paper towel," she said, trying not to dry heave.

He opened the towel. She looked away. "Squeamish?" She could hear the smile in his voice.

"I'm not used to examining cat vomit."

"It's my job. Here, look. Don't be shy." He showed her a compact, sausage-shaped cluster of hair, which he extracted from the mass of half-digested food. "It's a hairball."

"Oh. Really?" He would tell this story for years, the one about the clueless woman who didn't know the difference between acute food poisoning and a hairball.

"There are two kinds of hairballs. One kind is formed at the back of the cat's throat, the other in the stomach or small intestine."

She tried not to retch again. "Is it dangerous?"

"It's healthy for her to clean the hair out of her system now and then. But hairballs as big as baseballs have been found in the stomachs of some cats. Not that you need to worry about that. You could brush her regularly. That might help."

"You mentioned that." She leaned against the counter, feeling a bit lightheaded. "Two days ago, I never would've imagined that I'd be standing here in the night, next to a veterinarian, both of us examining a hairball. I never pictured having a cat in the shop."

He nodded thoughtfully. "Yeah, life can throw you."

"I feel silly."

"Aw, you didn't know." He dropped the hairball in the

garbage. "I'll take another look at the kitty and make sure she's okay, so you can sleep easy."

Did she ever sleep easy anymore? "I appreciate your help."

He was already heading back down the hall, but this time he stopped in the front room and looked around in the dimness. "This where you sell the dresses?"

The shop seemed somehow inert in the darkness, like a movie scene waiting for lights. "This is it, what there is of my livelihood."

"You sell men's clothes, too?"

"In a section along the south wall." She followed his gaze to the male mannequin.

"I like that jacket."

Her heartbeat kicked up, and she realized the jacket, designed and worn by Josh, just might fit Dr. Cole. "It's one of a kind."

"I need a suit for the veterinary conference next month. Can you believe I don't have a single suit that still fits?" He patted his belly, which looked firm to her. "Maybe I could find something here."

"I have limited inventory, but what I do have is unique."

"Maybe I can try that one on?"

"The one on the mannequin?"

"Yeah, why not?"

She felt a strange jolt. The jacket held too many memories. On their seventh anniversary, Josh had surprised her by taking her dancing at the Bayside Lounge in San Francisco. Now she remembered the evening as if it had happened only the night before—the scents of perfume and alcohol, the feel of his arm around her waist, his minty breath on her cheek.

But the jacket could fit Dr. Cole. She could make a sale. She fought a quick, silent war with herself, then she said, "I should've pinned a note to that one. It's only a display model. I'm afraid the jacket is not for sale. But, if you give me your size, I'll look through the rest of my inventory. I'm sure I can find the perfect suit for you."

"Perfect, huh? I'll hold you to that."

"Do you know your size?"

"I can check one of my suits, but they're all tight."

"I would need to take your measurements then."

"Then I'll have to come back."

"You will." For a moment, they looked at each other, then he went upstairs to check on the cat one more time before leaving.

Chapter Sixteen

Lily

After Dr. Cole left, Lily could not sleep. She thought about a suit for him. What would work? Not a brown silk sports jacket. She couldn't picture him with a fake tan, swinging a golf club. Not the gray flannel or seventies black polyester. Nothing mod. Nothing disco.

In bed, the cat curled up at her feet, not making a sound, and in the morning, the kitty woke first, sitting on Lily's chest and pressing a paw into her cheek.

Lily sat up, blinking, trying to clear the fuzz from her

brain. She'd dreamed of cutting up her wedding dress while Ida cheered her on.

Downstairs, the cat sat on the newspaper and knocked over Lily's teacup, spilling liquid all over the obituaries. The first advertisement for the shop hid in the bottom right-hand corner of page seven. Would anyone see it? Perhaps she should've bought a bigger spot. This morning, she planned to post *Found Cat* flyers all over town. She was creating the poster on her computer when Paige Williams waltzed in wearing a bright floral raincoat and boots, flashing her usual sunshine smile.

"I hear you have a cat in here," she said in her perky voice. "With two different-colored eyes, no less!" She whipped off her raincoat, revealing a pink cashmere sweater and a clingy black wool skirt.

"News gets around fast." Lily clicked the mouse to close the computer file. "How can I help you today?"

Paige looked around. "I might need a dress for a reception." The cat trotted straight over to a deep emerald evening dress, one of Josh's best creations. Paige's gaze followed. "Oh. My. Ida was right!"

"You spoke to Ida?" Great, the poor woman was spreading word of her mishap.

"She stopped by my office, said something about the cat showing her a dress that had to be cut right off her, but she insisted that the cat had a message. She's on some kind of liquid and fruit diet now."

"Oh, I feel terrible. I didn't mean to—"

"She's always looking for messages from the universe. She's like that, you know." Paige rushed over to the emerald dress. "What do you think? Will I look good in this?"

"It's one-of-a-kind formalwear. Hand-sewn inseams."

"I'll try it on. Thank you for showing this to me, kitty." Paige carried the dress into the fitting room. When she emerged, the dress looked almost right on her—but it didn't quite fit.

She turned sideways and examined her profile. "What's with the sizing? How can this be too small?"

Oh no, not again.

"Sizes are all different, depending on the year of manufacture and the brand name. A size sixteen from the fifties might be a size eight today."

Paige sighed and stared at some distant, happy moment. "It's so much like the dress I wore on my honeymoon. I felt like anything was possible."

"What do you mean? You don't think anything is possible now?"

Paige shrugged. "Oh, you know, I'm older now. Jaded. I was idealistic when I was young. I didn't even think about the fact that I was young. You only think about it when you get older. Maybe I assumed my youth would last forever. I thought love could be forever, too. I saw all these people around me breaking up, and I thought it would never be me. I was so much in love. I thought I could excel in my job and get rich, too, but here I am, cobbling together a living from two different jobs. Sometimes we have to face the limits of what is possible, don't you think?"

"I know what you mean, but you're not old. You're a breath of fresh air," Lily said.

Paige gave her a grateful smile. "Nice of you to say."

"I mean it, and I still believe anything is possible. Maybe life gets harder, but . . . just because your husband acted like a jerk, it doesn't mean life ends for you. You deserve better. There is always something new around the corner."

"For you, too," Paige said, her eyes bright. "Don't you think? Don't you want to find someone again? I mean, your husband passed over a year ago, didn't he?"

How had the conversation shifted back to Lily? "He did, and I don't know—maybe I'm not ready. I suppose I'm married to this shop right now. And the dresses inside. My husband designed this one for a local production of *West Side Story*."

"You mean it was a costume? That makes it even more special." Paige glanced out at the window display across the street. "Nice stuff in that shop, but the clothes don't have character."

"That's what I think, too, but don't tell anyone." Lily felt a warm rush of satisfaction.

Paige turned in a complete circle in front of the mirror. A spark of yearning came into her eyes. She looked at the cat, who sat on a nearby table, her rear end dangerously close to a folded silk scarf. "I do need something special like this," she whispered to the cat. "I'm going to my ex-husband's wedding. Can you believe it? I know the divorce was partly my fault. He was a jerk, but I played my part. I own up to that."

Lily froze in place, no words coming to mind. How could she respond to such a personal confession? "His wedding! I can understand your reluctance to go."

A single tear trickled down Paige's nose. "I mean, I know he cheated and everything. I want to put the past behind me. But now, yes, John's getting married and I—"

"You want to look good."

"I don't know why I'm telling you all this. The kitty is easy to talk to, don't you think? Cats don't judge you. They don't talk back. They don't argue. They don't give you advice."

Lily couldn't dispute that. "I have to admit, I talk to the cat, too. Sometimes I don't even realize I'm doing it."

"I bet she keeps a lot of secrets. If only she could talk. Or maybe she wouldn't want to."

The cat squinted at her, and Paige took a deep breath. "What do you say, kitty? The dress doesn't fit. I wish it did, but it doesn't. There you go."

Lily saw, now, how the emerald dress *could* fit Paige. She could add lace along the waist and neckline, perhaps a triangle of black. "I could . . . make some adjustments." Had Lily just spoken aloud?

Paige's face brightened. "Really? You could?"

"I've done a little sewing. I'll need to take your measurements. I'll be right back." Lily's heart pounded as she rushed behind the partition and into her makeshift office. What was she doing? Where did she keep the cloth tape measure? Did she even have one anymore? Could she remember how to take measurements?

She found an old tape measure in the bottom desk drawer, grabbed a pencil and paper, and returned to the shop. As she measured Paige's waist, hips, bust, chest, and neck, her training returned like old whispers. *Chest measurement is above the nipple, under the armpit. Waist—bend to one side, measure at the deepest wrinkle.*

"The sleeves are tight," Paige said.

"I can add a gusset, a diamond of dark fabric beneath the armpit, to increase the size of the sleeve."

"That's an ingenious idea."

"Nobody will ever know, even if you raise your arms above your head."

"The waist is so small. If I bend over, I can't breathe."

"I can add a triangle of fabric to take out the waist."

The cat still sat on the table, sphinx-style, watching through half-closed eyes.

"But I wouldn't want you to ruin the dress just for me."

"It won't be ruined, but I'll tell you what—you can pay me when the work is done. If you like it, great. If you don't, you don't need to buy it."

"Oh, I don't know what to say."

When Paige was ready to leave, Lily handed her a list of the proposed alterations.

"How much will this cost?" Paige asked, looking at the list.

"I'm not sure—I haven't done this before. But we can work something out."

"I should give you a deposit." Paige fumbled in her purse for her wallet, dropped it on the rug. Several cards and a small photograph fell out and fanned across the floor. The cat trotted over and sniffed at the snapshot.

Paige bent down to pick up the cards. The photo was of a tiny boy, a little clone of her but with dark hair.

"My son, Johnny," she said, showing Lily the photo.

"I didn't know you had a son! He's cute."

"He doesn't live with me. His dad has custody." She slipped the picture back into her wallet and looked at Lily with haunted eyes.

"The one who's getting married. The jerk?"

"Infidelity doesn't make you a bad parent, apparently." She smiled wanly. "But I . . . Anyway, it's little Johnny's idea—he wants me to go to the wedding, otherwise I wouldn't go. I miss him so much. I wish—never mind."

"Don't you get to see him?"

"Every second weekend, but it feels like every second year, or every second decade. More like every hundred years."

"I can imagine how awful that must be. Oh, Paige—"

"I'm okay." She retrieved a tissue from her purse and dabbed at the corners of her eyes. "I owe you one."

"You don't owe me anything," Lily said, but Paige was already heading for the door. After she left, Lily made another list, her answer to confusion. Sewing machine, thread, pinking shears, scissors, safety pins, seam ripper, tailor's chalk, straight pins, thimbles, needle, iron. Why had she offered to do this? This hadn't been in the plan, alterations to Josh's creations, or cutting a dress off a woman.

And yet.

She felt strangely buoyant, hopeful, her mind hovering somewhere above her body as she prepared to begin alterations. This was something she could do, something at which she had always excelled. She could picture the end result in her mind, Paige resplendent in the emerald dress, gliding up to her ex-husband, wowing him with her beauty and, as the renewed, unobtainable woman, she would breeze right past him.

Lily began to picture the window display in a new light, too. So, maybe she did not have a mannequin that could lie on its side, or expensive neon signs, but her clothes told stories, and what did that mean? Her display could tell a story, too. The story of an evening—two people meeting in a restaurant, sharing a bottle of wine, making a new start together.

As she worked to recast the display, the male mannequin watched her, but it seemed slightly different now— less like a receptacle for Josh's spirit, and more like an inanimate statue with opaque, unseeing eyes.

Chapter Seventeen

Kitty

As Lily flits around the shop with new determination, the spirits come out to watch. A young ballerina, who has been dead nearly twenty years, yanks a leotard off a hanger. She doesn't have the strength to pick it up off the floor. She believes she still has a body, muscular legs meant for pirouettes and pas de chats, a step of the cat. What remains of her, a mere thought the size of a marble but invisible, bounces from wall to wall, having slipped into the shop in a pair of vintage ballet slippers.

I sit on top of the shelves to groom my fur and observe

the commotion. Across the street, an elegant woman, all dressed in silk, is setting up a sign on the sidewalk. She and another woman are arranging racks of clothes and pots of flowers in front of the other shop. Lily is working so hard, she doesn't notice what's going on, and she doesn't see the inky spirit pushing a mannequin a few inches across the floor.

Now I discern the shape that the spirit wants to remember, the corporeal body she has lost. She was tall and thin, stooped and old. She was a sad woman, too, but she lost all hope. She wallowed here in this cottage, hiding on her own, pining for her lost love, and she does not want Lily—or anyone else—to remain here. She wants only to be left alone.

Chapter Eighteen

Lily

"What is this weird thing? A Halloween disco costume?"

Bish pulled a satin jacket off a hanger and held it up by finger and thumb, as if it were a dead rodent dangling by its tail. The cat sat at Bish's feet, gazing upward and batting at the shiny fabric.

"The real question is, what kind of weird thing is *that?*" Lily pointed at Bish's blue-and-black-striped leggings. At least she'd heard of the word "disco," so there was still hope for the girl.

"These are totally in style." Bish held out her right leg

and pointed her toes. She wore black shoes and when she frowned, she mildly resembled her morose father. "I bought these leggings across the street, like, last year."

"Of course you did." Lily tried not to sound bitter.

"Sorry, does that make you mad?" Bish sounded hopeful.

"Why would it? I wasn't even here last year."

"Oh, yeah, that candy shop was here. Too bad it's gone. Not too bad. I mean, I'm glad you're here now with all this old stuff. But I liked their Australian licorice."

"Maybe I should carry licorice instead of vintage clothing." Why had she focused only on the cottage when she'd first arrived? She hadn't given the other boutique a second thought. She'd worked in the yard, cleaning the flower beds, scrubbing and refilling the birdbaths, and fixing the squirrel feeder—as much as she could do in autumn. She'd thought a pretty garden would attract customers, but she hadn't anticipated the power of longevity and reputation. Somehow, people believed in The Newest Thing, and while a few had stopped in to look at her inventory, her shop had not yet caught on.

She knew success would take time, but she was growing impatient. How could Bish worry about a disco jacket when the entire population of Shelter Island seemed to be descending upon The Newest Thing, drawn by the *Semi-Annual Sale* sign?

"I still think you need more mirrors and a bigger sign out there like that banner." Bish pointed across the street.

"How did all those people know to go over there, though, before they even saw the banner?" Lily rearranged the wineglasses in her window dinner scene. Didn't anyone notice the voluptuous female mannequin, dressed in Sue Wong and flirting with the fiberglass male decked out in Armani?

"This should go to the thrift shop," Bish said, hanging up the jacket. "But if you want to keep it—"

"It's classic," Lily said, still looking out the window. "Didn't you ever see *Saturday Night Fever*?"

"My dad liked that old movie. He liked the dancing, but he doesn't want me to go to the Homecoming dance. Hypocrite. If I go, he wants me home early. He won't even let me wear the kind of dress my friends are wearing. He says it's as small as a postage stamp. I hate him."

"Hate is a strong word." Lily could remember using it when she was young and volatile, too. "He's probably trying to keep you from losing your virginity too soon."

Bish rested her hands on her hips. "How do you know I haven't already lost it?"

"Oh no. Have you?"

"None of your business." Bish stuck out her bottom lip, which made her look childlike. "But sometimes I do hate my dad. It's a lot more than that . . . more than the stupid dress."

"What is it then?"

"Never mind. You don't even know. Can I do my homework here with the kitty? You're keeping her. Cool."

"I'm not keeping her—didn't you see the flyers? I posted them all over town."

"She needs a better name. How about Trouble? Angel? MeowMeow? Edwina Scissorpaws?"

"Very creative, but she seems to like 'kitty' just fine."

"She does not. She wants a *real* name. Catpernicus."

"It's kitty until her owner claims her."

"Fine, whatever." Bish plopped onto the couch that Lily had dragged out from the back room.

"Florence must send out mailings to everyone, postcards or flyers announcing the sale," Lily went on, still looking across the street, trying to ignore the sinking sensation in her stomach. The sky had cleared, and now steam rose from rooftops and fence posts in the sunshine.

Bish swung one dangling foot. "They have a sale twice a year and everybody goes. She's cleaning out all the summer stuff to make room for winter. The longer the sale goes on, the cheaper everything gets. Maybe some of those people will come in here."

"Some already have, but not many." Lily thought of the

bird-like man who'd spotted the cat in the window and had come in looking for a crinoline petticoat, supposedly for his sister. He bought a lace number in his own size, and as he paid for the dress, he asked Lily how he should wash it. He quickly corrected himself, his face bright red. *I mean, how should my sister wash it?* Then there was Maude Walker, a perfectly round woman, also drawn by the cat, who imparted advice about the proper method for brushing the cat's teeth, keeping her coat clean, and preventing hairballs by giving her dollops of butter. During the long lulls, Lily rearranged the rooms, clearing spaces and bringing in the couch. She had planted attractive shrubs along the path, but nothing seemed to bridge the distance between the road and the porch.

A few minutes later, an elegant willowy woman came out of the shop across the street. Something in her confident demeanor, in the flow of her violet pantsuit and the glint of gold jewelry, made Lily certain that the woman was Florence. So she had shown up for her big sale. She was like an ethereal goddess of indeterminate age, her russet hair stylishly coiffed. She smiled and waved at customers as she adjusted the dresses hanging on the outdoor racks beneath the eaves. She glanced across the street and went back inside.

A cloud crossed over the sun, casting momentary darkness into Lily's shop. Bish picked up the cat and cradled her. "So what are you going to do? You could charge admission, you know, like a museum. You could make some money that way." She grinned, and Lily's skin prickled.

"That does it," she said. "Get up and help me. This means war." She hated to think this way, as if she needed to compete, but a few customers trickling in here and there, and alterations to Paige's dress, would not be enough to pay the bills.

"What do you want me to do?" Bish said, looking worried.

A moment later, she was helping Lily carry a rack of the best coats, sweaters, and slacks out to the sidewalk. The porch steps and the stone walkway seemed to go on forever. As Bish and Lily maneuvered the metal rack, the hangers shifted and clanged, the clothes sliding down to Bish's end, which she held lower than Lily's side.

"This isn't a good idea," Bish whispered to Lily.

"Why not?" Lily said. "Look."

"But—"

"Bish, just help me. No more advice for now, okay?"

"Whatever you say." Bish shook her head as they placed the rack on the sidewalk. Customers looked over and began to drift across the street.

"See?" Lily said out of the corner of her mouth, smiling at the first customer. "Come on, one more."

Bish helped her bring out one more carousel of clothing. It was working. People had begun to notice Past Perfect, and they noticed the cat in the window, and they came inside. The shop had become visible, emerging from the mist. Something had shifted in the air. Lily had reached out to the sidewalk, and now people were giving her a chance.

A young boy, no older than seven, came in with his mother and sat on the carpet and read to the cat from a hardcover picture book while his mother browsed. The cat sat right in front of him, her eyes half closed, as if she were listening, a blast from the heating vent ruffling her fur.

Lily imagined a whole gaggle of children in the shop, gathering around to read to the cat while their mothers—and a few fathers—bought up her entire inventory. What if she put children's books in the window? Even children's clothing? She was so busy re-imagining her shop that she failed to notice how quickly the sky had darkened.

So when Bish burst into the shop, her hair plastered to her head, dripping rain, it took Lily a moment to register what was happening.

"Flash squall!" Bish said, gasping for breath. "We need

to bring in the racks right now. Right this very second. Do you have some kind of tarp?"

But Lily had nothing except her raincoat, which did a lousy job of covering her precious woolen sweaters. Across the street, the sale racks at The Newest Thing flapped in the rising wind, but the overhanging eaves protected them, and Lily felt stupid for not having anticipated such a rapid change in the weather.

"Dammit, dammit!" she shouted as she and Bish carried the racks inside. She could imagine Florence watching from across the street.

"I tried to tell you," Bish said.

"But it was sunny."

"A sun break," Bish corrected her. "In the fall up here, it's always a sun *break*. You have to get to know the weather. Sunny one minute, flash flood the next."

"Why didn't you say so?"

"I tried." Bish grinned, water dripping from her nose. "So now we're going to the estate sale, right?"

"I wasn't planning on it, but . . . " The rain came down in sheets and suddenly turned to hail. The cat gazed at the ceiling, her ears twitching as ice pellets bombarded the roof.

"But what? We need to get replacement stuff. These clothes are history. They're, like, ruined."

"Not quite yet." But as Lily removed the wet clothes from the racks, she realized she might not be able to salvage the wool and silk. She thought she could hear someone laughing behind her, but when she turned around, nobody was there.

Chapter Nineteen

Lily laid out the woolen sweaters to dry, and although they weren't completely ruined, they were misshapen. How could she have been so foolish? Everyone in town must've known the weather might change. She stood out as the foreign immigrant to a stormy, unpredictable island.

But despite her embarrassing faux pas, the sidewalk sale had brought Past Perfect into the light. Shop traffic increased, partly due to the cat—whose otherworldly presence attracted a range of unusual and eccentric, cat-loving customers—and partly due to Lily's unusual and eccentric inventory.

Some dresses came with pictures of the original owners, perhaps their life stories as well. A silk gown, heavy with glass beading, had been made in Paris and worn during a honeymoon in Rome. A blue chiffon dress had lived on a farm for years, and a pink number had belonged to a woman named Cecilia, who'd worn the dress to church every Sunday. A handmade shirt, appliquéd with imported fabric, whispered of its history in post–World War II Germany. Lily imparted her special knowledge to her customers, explaining the difference between a bandage dress and a shift dress, for example, and she displayed a floral print tea dress in the window beside a summer picnic tableau. People were surprised to learn unusual trivia, like the story of the famous artist who'd once buried clothes and left them to decompose in his garden. He'd pulled them out and presented them as a radical new collection to the fashion industry, creating the famous "buried dress." Another designer had made a gown covered entirely in LED lightbulbs.

A few days after the sidewalk sale, when Lily had almost finished alterations to Paige's emerald dress, Vanya came in. She wore an oversized woolen coat, her yellow hair pulled back. Her belly seemed larger than before, her face bloated.

"The cat looks happy," she said. "I'm glad you still have her." She reached out to pet her, but the cat trotted away, nose sniffing the air, as if she understood where Vanya had come from.

"Don't take it personally," Lily said. "You probably smell like the clinic."

"Such is my lot. I can never wash that place away! Nice shop you've got here. It's good to get out. I've been putting in some long hours at the clinic."

"Let me know if I can help you." Lily kept her distance. She'd never liked salespeople who hovered, but she did not want to seem indifferent.

Vanya tried on loose dresses and sweaters and began to create quite a pile in the fitting room. As she browsed, her cheeks gained some color, and her eyes shone.

Retail therapy, Lily thought. Trying on clothes could have a palliative effect on the soul. "How are things at the clinic anyway?" she asked. "Is Dr. Cole working you too hard?"

"My husband thinks I should quit my job, just until, you know." Vanya patted her belly. "But I love what I do. I have to work to get my mind off things. And I need the money. My husband doesn't understand, but Dr. Cole really appreciates what I do."

"He should." Lily could not imagine Dr. Cole expressing his appreciation for anyone.

"He's a good doctor." Vanya pulled a folded slip of paper from her purse and slid it across the counter. "This is the bill for the house call. I almost forgot to give it to you."

Lily blushed. How much had Dr. Cole told Vanya? Had he mentioned the hairball? "Thanks. I meant to ask about it."

"He told me to send it to you, but I figured I was coming in here, so—"

"It was nice of you to stop by."

"I wanted to check out your shop anyway. I like what you've done. It has a homey feeling."

"Homey, I like that, too."

Vanya fumbled in her purse and brought out a beaded wallet. "Look, I'm sorry if he was rude to you, when you brought the cat into the clinic. I hope he was nicer when he came over here in the night."

"Sort of," Lily said. "But I woke him."

"He's changed since his wife left, but who can blame him? He loved Altona so much."

"I didn't know about that—about his wife leaving." A piece of surprising news. Lily busied her fingers, punching up the price for each garment in Vanya's pile. And what kind of a name was Altona?

"They went everywhere together. They were inseparable." Vanya shook her head sadly.

"He's divorced, then." Lily kept her voice steady, but her insides turned over. He'd been in her house, in her kitchen, in her bedroom, looking at her bra. He'd been single the whole time. Single and angry and damaged, missing his ex-wife.

Vanya produced a few crisp, twenty-dollar bills from her wallet. "He would have gifts sent to her at work. Flowers, gloves, jewelry."

"That's romantic," Lily said. She could hardly imagine him acting that way, giving anyone a gift. "I'm so sorry things didn't work out for the two of them." Poor Bish had been abandoned by her mother, too.

"It was sudden. But come to think of it, Altona liked to travel. She always seemed kind of . . . restless. I've been working for Doc for five years, and she left only last year. He hasn't been the same, like I said." Vanya put the money on the counter.

Lily picked it up, counted the bills, opened the register. "Of course he hasn't. When you've loved someone—"

"He even went a little crazy after she left, but he's more settled now."

"What do you mean, he 'went a little crazy'?" Lily

imagined him racing all over town, shouting, wielding an ax. Had she allowed a crazy ax murderer, driven insane by his wife's departure, into her cottage in the middle of the night?

"Oh, he just, you know. He went on a bunch of dates. Let's put it that way. Didn't get involved with anyone, though." Vanya looked around the shop, as if the clothes might be listening, and lowered her voice. "Some people go their whole lives pining for someone they've lost, but others can go right ahead and get remarried. Dr. Cole is definitely the pining type. He tried not to be. When my great uncle died, my great aunt got remarried almost right away, at the ripe age of sixty-seven."

"Sixty-seven is not old these days," Lily said, handing back Vanya's change.

"Her second husband was eighty. They went trekking in the Himalayas together. Now, I love my husband, but if he died, I would probably find someone else pretty quickly, too."

"Do you really mean that?"

"I only mean, my husband and I, we don't have the perfect marriage, but then, every marriage has its stresses, right? Were you ever married? Then you would know." Vanya pushed a strand of straight, yellow hair behind her ear. How could anyone's hair be so very yellow, like the petals of a spring daisy?

"I was married. He died." The word "died," hovered in the air, then popped like a bubble.

"Oh. Wow. I'm sorry." Vanya's eyes widened and her expression shifted fluidly from stunned surprise to pity to carefully modulated sympathy. Lily had grown accustomed to this multifaceted response, and she understood that she had now stepped across an invisible threshold from being just another person to having the word "widow" plastered across her forehead.

"Thanks," she said politely. "I'm doing fine." A lie. Only the night before, she'd dreamed that Josh was humming downstairs in the kitchen, making scrambled eggs. When she'd woken, she'd realized the humming was the cat purring. The smell of eggs came from a restaurant down the block; she had left the window open. She'd discovered that while the first floor of the cottage had drafty spots, the heat rose into the bedrooms.

She began to fold the clothes and put them in a large paper shopping bag with handles. Perhaps when Vanya walked out carrying the bag, customers in The Newest Thing would look across the street, and they would want to be in on the action.

"What type are you?" Vanya said, taking the bag.

"Excuse me?"

"Are you the type to move on, or the type to keep pining?"

"Is there another option? All right. I think I might be the pining type. I did go on a couple of dates about six months after my husband died, but they didn't work out."

Vanya tilted her head quizzically. "Okay, spill. What happened?"

"Well, one was a blind date that a friend set up for me. He turned out to have obsessive-compulsive disorder, had to keep getting up from the table to wash his hands. I counted five times during dinner, a few more times after."

Vanya laughed. "And what about the second date? Was it any better?"

"He was a nice man, but he wanted to get me into bed right away, saw me as desperate or something, but it was too soon."

"Oh, I see. But maybe sex isn't so bad. My husband and I still, you know." Vanya patted her belly again and lowered her voice. "Doctor says it's okay."

Lily's cheeks heated. Too much information. "Um, that's—"

"Sex can be a healer. Why don't you go for Dr. Cole?

When I first started working at the clinic, I had, like, this huge crush on him. I was so jealous of Altona."

"I'm sure that happens fairly often, an employee developing a crush on her boss." Lily tidied the receipts in the register drawer.

"Everyone had a crush on him, and I mean everyone. Something about him being inaccessible, I think. But you got to see him in the night, right here. You're lucky."

"It wasn't a date!" Lucky to have a brooding, desolate man in her house? "The cat had a hairball."

"Yeah, he told me. Funny." Vanya looked over at the cat and winked. "She has hairballs, pretty typical. Well, I'd better get back to work. You both have a nice day. I'll be back."

"Tell all your friends—about my shop, not the hairball!" Lily called out as Vanya maneuvered her belly out the door. Just as she was leaving, a stooped gentleman came in, looking around with a tentative expression. Lily recognized him as a ferry worker who loaded and unloaded cars on the Seattle run, only he seemed bare without the bright orange vest, like a tree in winter. Thin and long-limbed, he wore shades of gray that matched the sky.

The cat trotted over to him, somehow knowing that he would be friendly, that he would kneel to pet her with affection. Lily thought him handsome in a gaunt, understated way, but the moment the reaction came to her, she caught a glimpse of a man standing across the street. It was Josh, staring in at her, untouched by the rain, his eyes sad. In the instant, she remembered the first time he had held her hand, the first time they had walked the beach just north of San Francisco, where they'd seen a gray whale spouting offshore. She remembered their first kiss on that beach at sunset, a moment charged with electricity. It all rushed through her, taking her breath away. *I'm sorry, Josh. It will always be you. How can it be otherwise?*

A passing car obscured her view, erasing Josh, as if he'd never been standing there.

"Do you have a suit for a funeral?" the gaunt man was asking her. "And I don't want anything black."

Chapter Twenty

Lily

"Just a moment, sir. I'll be right with you."

Lily knew she seemed distracted and crazy, but she had to run across the street, to see where Josh had gone. As she hurried down the sidewalk in her running shoes, she felt the cold rain on her face. The bushes rustled in the wind, shop awnings flapping. She heard metal clanging on the town dock down the street, smelled the dank odors of the beach at low tide. She stopped in the spot where she had seen Josh. Here on the sidewalk, right in front of The Newest Thing, she could see into the front window of her own shop. Soft lights illuminated the mannequins, which appeared to be backlit silhouettes. Then the cat hopped into the window, a pale aura surrounding her.

Lily looked right and left. No sign of Josh. The rain was seeping through her sweater to her T-shirt. She had imagined him. She had hallucinated. But he had seemed real. Maybe his spirit had really been here. Such things happened.

She ran back into the warmth of her shop. The dust on the countertop looked slightly disturbed, as if someone had run a finger across its surface. She shivered and turned her attention to the new customer.

"Sorry about that," she said, wiping the water from her face. "I had to go out and see something."

The man nodded, glancing out the window, then returned to browsing.

"I'm sorry you have to go to a funeral," she went on. "There's no rule about wearing black. I didn't wear black to my husband's memorial service, but only because he didn't want me to. He mentioned wanting people to wear bright colors and dance at his funeral. But he didn't realize he would die so soon." Why had she just told all this to a complete stranger? Was it the rain and cold, messing with her mind? Would the man turn and run out of the shop, never to return?

His face softened and he came right up to her. "I'm sorry you lost him. So what color did you wear?"

"I wore a deep turquoise dress, not quite black but close enough." She smiled. *Sometimes, revealing a little of your pain, your vulnerability, can bring people closer to you,* she thought. "What color would you like to wear?"

"Maybe the cat will help me decide." He made for the south wall, glancing at the suit jacket on the male mannequin. "Maybe that one."

"It's just a display," she said quickly. "And too small for you." She had not heard from Dr. Cole since their nighttime encounter, which now seemed like a distant dream. Perhaps he'd mentioned needing a suit merely to be polite.

The cat stayed close to the gaunt man as he browsed, his long fingers touching the fabric with precise delicacy. Lily kept glancing at the road, but the image of Josh did not return.

The man was talking to the cat in a low voice. "Last time I wore a suit was at my graduation . . ." and ". . . don't even know what size . . ." and ". . . should wear my birthday suit . . ." The cat purred at him.

He pulled out a white suit. "Whoa, now that's an eyesore."

"That's a Palm Beach linen suit, circa nineteen thirties,

one of my oldest pieces. Probably not great for a funeral, even if you're steering clear of black."

He nodded, putting the suit back. "I bet you wouldn't wear a Palm Beach suit, huh, kitty? What's your name?"

"She's just kitty," Lily said. "And I'm Lily."

"I saw the flyers you posted in town. Looks as though the little kitty has settled in here pretty well."

"If her owner comes, she'll go home."

"She is home, I think. I'm Rupert, known as Rupe to those who love me." He pulled out a dark purplish-blue Jarvis suit. "This is perfect. The color of royalty, Willy Wonka, eccentricity and audacity and all that."

"Are you sure you want purple?"

"Why not? What kind of suit is this anyway?"

"Three-piece, fabric-covered buttons, polyester in a lightweight poplin weave."

"Looks like my size." While he tried on the suit, the cat waited outside the fitting room, as usual.

Rupert emerged looking surprisingly good in purple. "What do you think?" He tugged at the shoulders. "Michael said I should go to a men's specialty shop instead. They know how these things are supposed to fit, but I'm not sure."

"I can alter the suit for you." Lily wondered who Michael was, then realized Rupert and Michael were probably partners. She couldn't help but feel slightly disappointed, although she had no intention of getting involved with anyone.

Rupert gave her a skeptical look. "Michael says the men's tailors know better."

"I know a few things, too. You don't want the jacket to pull at the armpits. The padding in the shoulders is the right width. The jacket has a waist, and it's just the right length. It shouldn't go all the way to the thigh."

Rupert raised his brows at her in the mirror. "You've done this before. I'm impressed. Your prices are good, too."

Finally, she could imagine the shop teeming with people who trusted her nimble sewing, her understanding of fabric and alterations. "You need to choose the shoes you're going to wear at the funeral, or at least similar shoes."

"Then find me a pair. I wear a size twelve."

"And you can't wear that T-shirt underneath."

Measuring him in the suit, when he wore the right dress shirt and shoes, felt like a fluid dance with the tape measure and pins.

"The sleeve should break at the wrist," she said. "One slight crease in the pant, and it breaks just at the top of the shoe."

"Breaks," he said. "I like that word. Like a wave break-ing, makes me think of surfing."

"It's a term I learned in the industry." Could Florence say as much? When Lily had finished flitting around Rupert, pinning and measuring, they both looked out the front window. Florence's display had changed yet again. A new mannequin had appeared, this one in motion, legs bent, the woman leaning forward. She wore a knit cap and parka, two ski poles in hand. Florence stood in the win-dow, laying a blanket of fake snow.

"She's creative, I'll have to give her that," Rupert said, taking off the jacket and draping it across the counter next to Lily's coffee cup.

She forced a smile. "It doesn't snow on the island too often, does it?"

"Couple of times a year, but it melts after a few days. Most people head up to Mount Baker or some other mountain resort to ski. You ever been?"

"I prefer cross-country," Lily said, fussing with the price tag on the jacket. "I can have this ready for you in a couple of days. We should do a second fitting, make final adjustments."

"A second fitting! You are an expert!"

"Oh, I wouldn't say that, but if you like my work, do me a favor and tell your friends."

"I most certainly will."

Just as Rupert came out of the fitting room in his street clothes, the mailman waltzed in, decked out in blue rain gear, and dropped a pile of envelopes on the counter. He tipped his hat and left. On top of the pile was a glossy, oversized postcard bearing the logo of The Newest Thing, a watercolor pink dress on a hanger next to a matching purse, and the announcement: *Now offering New to You Clothing on Consignment.* What on earth?

Rupert must've caught her frowning at the postcard. "Recycling bin," he said.

"Why do you suppose they're doing that? Suddenly now, Florence is selling clothing on consignment?" Her voice rose to a shrill pitch. Her shop didn't even have a logo.

"Everybody's trying to make a living in this economy," Rupert said gently. "Just ignore it."

"But I thought The Newest Thing—"

"Listen, I know Florence. I've known her all my life. She's a good businesswoman. She's always trying new things. Clothing on consignment is probably selling better than her new clothes. And that is a good thing for you."

Selling better? What a joke. What could Florence possibly offer? What did she know about vintage clothing? How could she have the nerve to tread on Lily's territory? But should Lily even feel territorial? After all, maybe two shops would attract more bargain shoppers than one, right?

Would Lily have to carry new clothing now? She couldn't imagine such a thing. She and Josh had always talked about remaining true to their vision.

"Don't worry," Rupert said, patting her shoulder. "There is room enough in this world for all of us."

But was there? Lily watched a new sign go up in the window of The Newest Thing, in a font to match the words on the postcard. *Now Selling Clothing on Consignment.*

Beneath the postcard on the countertop, she found only bills—telephone, electricity, credit card, and the list went on. After Rupert left, she reached across the counter to pick up the purple suit, and her elbow knocked her coffee cup, spilling liquid all over the jacket, which she had so carefully pinned. How could her day get any worse? It could. Stepping into her shop was a woman she had last seen two years ago, a woman she had known when Josh was alive, a woman she had not expected to see again.

Chapter Twenty-one

Kitty

As the slight woman steps in across the threshold, the spirits bask in the glow of her beauty. I'm lovelier than anyone, but for a human, she is stunning, her platinum hair twisted up into a fancy do. She must have trouble grooming that getup.

The man who comes in behind her is smitten. He is square, as if made of a series of blocks. He doesn't know that the woman has secrets, and he has secrets of his own. The smells cling to their clothes, hair follicles, and beneath their fingernails. Their histories stick to the soles of their shoes. The woman smells of sidewalks and department stores, doctors' offices and perfume. The man smells of cologne and car exhaust and other women.

As they close the door, a blast of cold air blows in after them. Lily pretends to be busy laying out the wet clothes to dry, but everything about her is aware of these new intruders.

The inky ghost of the old woman slides over to the blocky man. She has mistaken him for her lost lover—the captain of a sunken ship. She touches his hair with her phantom hand, but she's not really touching him, only imagining that she is. He reaches up to run his fingers through his hair, perhaps sensing her nearby. His sculpting spray has fought a losing battle with the wind.

The inky spirit tries to grab his shoulder, and the man shivers. He closes his black umbrella and leaves it in the bin by the door. Lily can no longer ignore these visitors, so she turns around, strides up with squared shoulders, and puts on a bright smile.

The delicate woman pulls off her white gloves, smiles back with fake sweetness, and unbuttons the collar of her coat. Jewels glint on her neck, and I have an urge to leap.

"Lily, I'm so happy to see you." The woman reaches out to shake Lily's hand.

"Drew," Lily says. I can feel her mind hurtling back in time. "Wow, I didn't expect to see you. You look great."

"So do you," Drew fibs, withdrawing her hand. "You've lost weight. I heard you moved up here, out to some island."

"You found me!" Lily wants them to lose her again.

Drew turns to the man. "Dillon, this is Lily. Remember, I told you about her?"

"Good to meet you." The man nods, but he has left his attention elsewhere. The inky ghost moves off. I stay hidden beneath a rack of black dresses.

"Dillon's my husband," Drew says.

Lily nods, tension in her face. "You got married! Congratulations."

"Dillon's a partner with Dillon and Reed, you know, the law firm in downtown Seattle? I met him while I was on a trip up here to visit my cousin, and it was love at first sight."

"I see." I can tell Lily has never heard of Dillon & Reed. The word "reed" reminds me of a pond where some ducks were hiding in the reeds. "What brings you all this way?"

"Don't look so surprised!" Drew says. From here, I see the delicate underside of her nose, her slim legs, her high-heeled, shiny black rain boots. "I came looking for you. It took me a while. You're pretty far from everything."

"But it's easy to get here by ferry," Lily says.

"You moved all this way without telling anyone."

"Was I supposed to tell everyone?"

"Well, no, but . . . I was hoping you would stay in touch."

"I'm sorry I didn't."

"It doesn't matter. I've found you now. Dillon and I are looking for a house to buy on the eastside. We're renting a condo right now, but it's expensive. We want to settle down and have a yard, you know, for a family."

"Sounds lovely." Lily's tone says she wants them to leave, but Drew does not understand.

She turns to Dillon again. "Lily was married to Josh Vilmont, the designer I used to work for."

"Oh. Vilmont! Wow." Dillon's brows rise.

Lily swallows, and her body stiffens. "So what are you doing these days? Besides living in Seattle?"

"I've got my own company," Drew says. "I employ three designers. Drew Galt Designs. Maybe you've heard of us?"

"I might have," Lily says, lying. "Good for you."

"I also have a shop, two thousand square feet, and this is the real reason I came here." Drew breaks away from Dillon, leaving him like a boat adrift in an unfamiliar sea, and glides over to a glittering evening dress. "My shop is in the Green Lake area. I could use a good store manager, someone to take care of the books and such. You were so good with Josh's business."

"Our business."

"Of course—that's what I meant. So, what do you say?"

Lily is quiet. The man shoves his hands into his coat pockets, receptacles for his secrets—slips of paper and business cards with cryptic writing scrawled in ink and redolent of perfume and promises.

"You want to hire me," Lily says, "but I've got a shop of my own, as you can see."

"Of course, a lovely little place."

"My hands are full." Lily's so stiff now, she could be made of stone.

Drew goes back to rescue Dillon, slips her hand into his. "Why don't you at least consider my offer? You would be managing a bigger place with more foot traffic in a central location—"

"Thanks for the offer, but I'm not sure I want to move again."

"Maybe you want to stay here for another reason? New boyfriend or fiancé?"

"No, not at all."

"But you're having a little fun, aren't you? I know it was hard to lose Josh. We all loved him. But you must have a need to move on?"

"I am moving on."

"Have you been seeing anyone? I hear the Internet can produce good matches these days."

"I'm not much into computers."

Dillon examines his short cuticles. From this angle, I can see the hairs in his nose.

"Oh my goodness! What's that thing?" Drew has spotted me, oh no. She lets go of Dillon's hand, her face pale. "There's an animal in your shop."

"It's a cat," Lily says.

"You have a cat?" Drew comes over and peers down at me, frowning. Her perfume makes me sneeze. I can't help it if a little saliva sprays onto her cheek. She steps back and wipes her face.

"She's a girl," Lily says, a touch of a smile on her lips. "She's a good shop cat."

I stay very still, trying not to sneeze again.

Drew recovers her composure, although a little makeup has smeared on her cheek. "Shop cat, of course. I was just . . . surprised."

"You would allow a cat in your shop, wouldn't you?" Lily says.

Drew pats her hairdo and twitches her stunning, delicate nose. "I'm not much of an animal person, but I know many people are. Extremely unusual eyes. Kind of demonic."

"They look more angelic to me," Lily says.

Dillon comes over and looks at me, the foreign smells on him growing stronger as he approaches.

"One green eye and one blue eye," he says, peering closely at my face. Now is my chance. I jump up and bat at his pocket, my claws latching on, bringing out what I know is in there.

"Kitty, no!" Lily rushes over. "I'm so sorry. I can reimburse you for any damage to your suit."

"No problem. Don't worry about it." Dillon reaches for the slip of paper that I pulled from his pocket, the evidence lying on the floor, but in an instant, Drew picks up the paper and tucks it into her own pocket. Her expression hardens, but she does not look surprised. These indiscretions are not news to her, and yet . . .

Lily does not understand Drew's pain, the compromises she has always made, even before she met Dillon. She was in love with Lily's mate—hopelessly, sadly in love with a man who would never love her back. Her beauty was not enough. It was not enough to keep her absent father around through her childhood, not enough to make her mother love her instead of resenting her birth. Few people have ever looked beyond her surface. She is even envious of me, an animal so easily loved, or so she thinks.

"Well, we should be going," Drew says quickly. "The

cat is a . . . nice touch." She and Dillon are heading for the door.

"Thanks for stopping by," Lily calls out, following them. They leave in a rush, and the door swings shut.

Lily watches them take off down the sidewalk, her lips turned down. I wish I could tell her what I know, that she shouldn't envy Drew's life, that no matter how things look on the outside, they're rarely the same on the inside.

"Drew Galt Designs, huh?" Lily says in a thoughtful voice. I can tell by the look in her eyes that the encounter has shaken her, changed her—that something new is about to happen.

Chapter Twenty-two

After Drew and Dillon left, Lily felt light-headed, her mind racing. She'd thought she could escape the past by leaving San Francisco, but Drew had found her anyway, and unwanted reminders had blown in with her. Once, Lily had caught Drew leaning across the lunch table at the design studio, flirting with Josh. He'd been smiling as if the two of them shared some secret joke. Had he ever actually had an affair with Drew? Or at the very least, had he ever liked Drew the way she had obviously liked him?

Lily had brought up the subject over dinner, and Josh

had bristled. What else did he have to do, he'd said, to show her that he loved her? He already demonstrated his devotion every moment of every day. She had trusted him, believed him. She still did. But Drew's beauty had planted unwelcome seeds of insecurity, and when she had taken a design job at another firm, Lily had been relieved. But Drew kept popping up at trade shows and dinner parties, and once Lily had caught Drew looking at Josh across the table with a studied kind of hunger. He'd been the one to leave the party early, to tell Lily that he felt uncomfortable.

She had been sure of her marriage, and yet she'd resented having anyone even threaten her happiness one iota. How dare this woman come up here now, to stir up trouble all over again. Why couldn't she leave Lily to focus on the happiest memories? Did she resent Lily that much? Did she really want Lily to work for her, or did she only want to flaunt her new life?

Either way, Lily felt newly galvanized. By what, exactly, she didn't know. Anger or resentment—did it really matter? She felt a new sense of purpose.

She picked up the cat and kissed her furry head. How could anyone call her a "thing" or merely an "animal"? An insult to this cat was an insult to Lily's shop. In a short time, this little fluffy creature had become integral to Lily's business. Many people had come in looking for the cat, drawn by her mystical qualities, or perhaps by her unusual eyes. Perhaps they sought comfort, commiseration, or hope in an unpredictable world.

Lily had sought the same when she arrived on the island, and by buying the cottage on a whim, she had actually been making a calculated decision. She had always wanted to change her life, to leave the city. Had Josh's death merely freed her to follow her dream? Had it been a plan they had shared, or had the dream belonged to her alone?

Either way, she needed to consciously commit to her future. She had to accept the cat or leave her at the shelter, make the shop work or let it sink, move forward or stay forever stuck, as her mother had tried to warn her. Her poor mother, who still called every few days to make sure her daughter was still alive and well.

I'm more than well. I'm great, Lily thought. She would get to know the island people and the island for real—or leave them behind. There was no middle place.

She looked at Josh's jacket on the mannequin, the jacket that he would never wear again. Dammit, somebody needed to wear that thing. If it fit Dr. Cole, so be it. She called the animal clinic, her heartbeat kicking up. She shifted from foot to foot. Why was she so nervous? Was it because she now knew he was single? That every woman on the island had coveted him? That he'd slept around but had remained unattainable? Was it because he was still hopelessly in love with his ex-wife?

It was only a jacket on a mannequin, for goodness' sake.

"Island Animal Clinic," Vanya said at the other end of the line. "How can I help you?" Her voice came through bright and friendly, putting Lily at ease.

"Vanya, it's Lily."

"Oh, hey! I'm wearing the vintage blue sweater. Everyone says it brings out my eyes."

"It is a beautiful Chanel, perfect for you. Be sure to wash it by hand and don't put it in the dryer."

"I won't. I've been talking up your shop to everyone, too. You need a business card."

"I'm going to order them today. Um, I'd like to talk to Dr. Cole if he's around." She tried to sound casual, but her voice came out a little thin and strained.

"He's in with a client at the moment. Hold on." Vanya's voice became muffled as she covered the receiver. She said something to a client. A dog barked in the background, and Lily almost hung up, feeling ridiculous. *No, remember, move forward. Grit your teeth. This is your life.*

"So you want to leave a message for him?" Vanya said, coming back on the line.

Lily glanced out the window. The display in The Newest Thing was in the midst of another transformation, two mannequins—one male and one female—positioned in the window. Flo was about to adorn them in some new style, but for the moment, they were both unclothed.

"Yes," she said. "Tell him I need to measure him for the jacket, if he wants it. Otherwise I'll sell it to someone else. He can either call me back or come into the shop."

"I'm sure he'll be over when he can tear himself away from work."

"Thanks, Vanya."

When Lily hung up, she realized she had stepped across a threshold from which there might be no return.

The cat sat beneath a hat tree, staring up at nothing, giving Lily a sudden idea for a shop logo. A cat with her fur blowing in the wind, wearing a vintage hat.

She checked the Internet for images, sketched a variation on one, and on a crazy impulse, she bundled up and rushed out in the blustery day to Fairport Graphics, where she ordered a logo image, business cards, and postcards.

Then she removed the *Found Cat* flyers from corkboards and telephone poles, bulletin boards and windows. The cat was going to stay. Who cared if the she ripped a couple of dresses or went psycho in the night? Sometimes life could throw you, as Dr. Cole had said, and sometimes that was a good thing.

Chapter Twenty-three

Kitty

I wonder what has just happened to Lily? She returns to the shop light on her feet, her cheeks flushed. For the first time since I came inside, I feel a hankering to leave, to be free, to see what she saw, to feel what she felt. But then I remember the long nights in the wind and cold, my belly aching with hunger. Do I want that life again?

Anyway, I can't leave yet. Sadness lingers in her heart, and the spirit of Lily's former mate is growing stronger. He compresses and expands, disappears and reappears, as if unsure of the shape he's meant to take, or what he is meant to become.

When Paige stops in for her dress, he slowly fades into the wall, as if he has run out of energy, but I have a feeling he will be back.

In the altered getup, Paige looks like a mermaid I once saw emerging at low tide to bask in the moonlight. She was also clad in tight, shiny green, with similar pale skin.

Paige turns in front of the mirror, checking her reflection from all angles, lifting her arms, dropping them, spinning in a slow circle.

"Amazing, Lily. How did you do it?"

"I made a few small adjustments." Lily smiles, and I sense the warmth coursing through her.

"I'm a whole new person."

"I'm glad you like it."

"I love it."

Lily floats through the next couple of moon cycles, chattering to me about alterations, the sales she is making, the new window display. The sweet man, Rupert, returns to help her set up new display lights. Turns out, he's good with electronics and wires. He slips me freeze-dried chicken treats when Lily isn't looking. She fits him with a new purple suit, and he smiles and hugs her and they both spill water from their eyes.

"Michael thinks I'm insane to wear this color," Rupert says, modeling the suit. "But he's not allowed to have an opinion. He's not going with me to the funeral. He's off on another six-day shift, and I'm leaving for Virginia tomorrow."

"That's a long time apart. Do you miss him?" Lily asks.

"Like the devil. But the passengers love him. He's one of the few singing flight attendants who isn't tone deaf."

Lily nods, her mind elsewhere. She looks out the window as if searching for someone. Ah, yes, now I know who it is. He arrives rather suddenly the next morning. When he steps inside, her heartbeat taps all over the universe. But on the outside, she remains calm. The doctor is in regular clothes, bringing the cold air and the smell of the salty sea. This time, I know he's not here for me. He's here for the jacket on the mannequin, or so he says. When he tries it on, Lily fusses with the sleeves and the collar, while he stands there, looking at her in the mirror.

"I'll make some alterations and it will fit you perfectly," she says, fussing some more, not looking into his eyes.

He nods, changes into his regular clothes, shoves his hands into his pockets, hesitates. "I need to get Bish a little . . . something. I have no idea what she likes these days."

"You can't go wrong with jewelry. Here, come and take a look." She pulls a velvet display case from beneath the checkout counter.

The ghost of her former mate wafts down and wraps

around her as Dr. Cole leans over the jewelry. Lily points to a silver necklace with white beads.

"This is sterling." She hands the necklace to Dr. Cole. "It's a choker. Sits above the collarbone. Perfect for Bish."

I sit on the edge of the counter, my tail swishing, and look from Lily to the doctor and back.

"Whatever you say," he says. "Looks good to me."

"I might have a box." As she bends forward, her necklace slips out from beneath her sweater, the gold ring and vial of ashes dangling in full view.

Dr. Cole takes a step back.

Lily tucks the necklace beneath the pullover, her cheeks a bright shade of pink.

"No need for a box," Dr. Cole says, standing away from her now.

"It's no problem." Lily quickly arranges the silver necklace in a gift box, puts the box in a small paper bag. "Bish is going to love this."

"I'm sure she will." He takes the bag, then turns and heads for the exit. I can't let him leave, not with Lily's heartbeat going crazy. As he opens the door, I jump down, stagger across the floor, and let out a strangled, unearthly cry before collapsing dramatically on the carpet.

Chapter Twenty-four

Lily

What could have happened to the cat? Lily's worst night-mare had just come true. The moment she'd opened her heart to the little creature, the poor old "senior" cat had keeled over and died. Horrible scenarios rushed through Lily's head—the cat had suffered a stroke, a heart attack, or a rupture of a major artery. Or maybe her tiny body had finally given out. Maybe old cats died this way—they kept going for years and then winked off like a lightbulb.

That's what you get for loving someone again, and a fragile senior cat, no less. Lily went a bit numb with fear as she kneeled on the carpet next to the cat, who lay stretched out on her side, her breathing shallow. "What's wrong with her?" Lily said, knowing she sounded desperate. "Could this be another hairball, a bigger one stuck in her throat?"

"I don't think so. Did you see what happened?" Dr. Cole kneeled on the other side of Lily. She heard a cracking sound, maybe from his joints. "She was okay a minute ago."

"I have no idea. She just collapsed. You saw! You just petted her."

"But then I turned away." He put his ear down to the cat's chest, then he pulled back her upper lip to check her gums. "She's not cyanotic. See? Her gums are pink. She's breathing. Her heartbeat sounds all right."

"But she's obviously in distress! What's going on? Do something! You're the vet." Lily teetered on the edge of panic, but an inner part of her stood back, observing from a dispassionate distance.

Dr. Cole gave her a curious look, but he did not seem perturbed. "Exactly what happened? Did she fall?"

"She doesn't fall. She jumped off the table. She always does that. It's not a long way down. She can jump from much higher up and not hurt herself."

He pulled a tiny flashlight from his pocket and shone a pin of light in each of the cat's eyes. She squinted, and her pupils contracted. "Nothing wrong there. Her responses are normal."

Lily tried to think back through the past couple of days. "Could it have been the cantaloupe?"

"You gave her cantaloupe?"

Great, she had killed the cat with fruit. "I hope it's not toxic to cats. She was crying for it, so I figured—"

"A little cantaloupe is okay, but not a lot."

"I gave her only a spoonful."

He palpated her belly. "I don't feel anything unusual in her abdomen, but she should have an X-ray."

Lily's hands began to go numb. The last time this had happened was right after Josh's accident, when the telephone call had come from the trauma center. She'd thought she would never survive the drive to the hospital, yet somehow, she had made it. Now, she was getting into Dr. Cole's truck, holding the nearly comatose cat wrapped in a blanket in her arms. There hadn't been time to get the carrier.

Dr. Cole raced through downtown, right through a red light, as rain pelted the windshield. Somehow, even in her panic, the detached part of Lily noticed the interior of his truck. Unlike Josh, Dr. Cole was not a neat freak. The cab was a mess of papers and tissues, a jacket thrown on the seat next to a library book.

At the clinic, they rushed inside, the reception area

quiet and dark. Dr. Cole whisked the cat off, turning on lights as he went, leaving Lily to wait an eternity, trying not to bite her nails.

Fifteen minutes later, he came back. The cat lay in his arms, unmoving. This couldn't be happening. He was a veterinarian. He was supposed to save little animals in distress. The cat hadn't been in an accident. She hadn't shown any sign of illness. The universe was playing a sick, cruel joke. The room began to spin, and Lily sat down, the blood draining from her head, and realized that she was about to faint.

Chapter Twenty-five

Kitty

The doctor lets me down gently. Of course, I can't help landing on my feet. But I wobble a little, pretend I'm recovering from a terrible trauma. Shaky and slow, I tiptoe around the waiting room. My tail swishes back and forth, and I sniff every corner.

"So she's okay?" Lily says in a trembling voice. She's pale, a little grayish.

"She appears to be fine," Dr. Cole says. "Do you need some water?"

"No, I'm okay. She's not sick? She looked . . . I mean . . ."

"She's not sick as far as I can tell."

I trot over to Lily and purr, rubbing against her legs.

"You crazy cat! I'm going to kill you!" Lily tries to sound angry, but her tone betrays her relief. She scoops me into her arms, nearly collapsing my lungs. "You scared me to death!"

Not to death, exactly. She's still very much alive, but I may not be for long if she keeps squeezing me so hard. She kisses the top of my head. "It's a miracle. Thank you, thank you. How did you save her?"

She puts me on the floor again. I give myself a good shake and set about cleaning my fur.

Dr. Cole smiles, and a sliver of light enters the dark room inside him. "She made a remarkable recovery all by herself."

"Maybe it was the quiet in here?"

Dr. Cole looks around, as if feeling the silence for the first time. "It is pretty quiet. No dogs and cats making noise in the kennels."

"You have kennels?"

He jabs his thumb toward the back of the clinic. "I can show you if you're interested."

"Definitely."

They look at each other, and a moment later, he scoops me up and tucks me under his arm, and Lily is following us through a swinging door into a back hall. He gives her the complete tour of the pharmacy room, break room, and grooming table, then points toward the surgery suite. Lily peeks through the tiny window in the door. "Must've taken you a long time to learn how to use all that equipment."

"We learn five species. Not just one."

"Have you ever had an animal die on the operating table?"

"Doesn't happen often, but we did have one cat react to anesthesia a few years ago. We tried to revive him, but we weren't successful. This is very rare."

The moment stays with him, like the other memories and darkness knocking around inside him.

"I'm sorry. Was it awful?"

"I got emotional, yeah, and I've been practicing for over twenty years." He scratches me on the head. "Emotional burnout is a major reason people leave this profession."

"Are you burned out?"

"In a way. I'm thinking of going part time, giving my colleague the extra hours."

"What do you do to unwind?"

"I hike, play guitar, read. But my job can also be incredibly satisfying when I've helped someone. Just yesterday, a desperate client brought in her papillion. He hadn't been eating for two days. An ultrasound revealed a gall bladder problem that would've killed him. But we did surgery right away and saved his life."

Papillion, a breed of dog with ridiculously gigantic ears but a weak sense of hearing.

"That must be an amazing feeling," Lily says.

He nods, still holding me under his arm. "It can also be overwhelming. I try to get out and enjoy the air." He opens a door into a back room with a concrete floor and several large, long cages. The smell of dog grows too strong in here. "These are the kennels. We stopped boarding cats here a while ago. They were right across from the dogs."

Lily nods, but she's frowning.

We leave the room, not a moment too soon, and head down another hallway that loops back around toward the front.

"I'll be right back," he says at an office door. "I need to return a client call. I won't be long." He hands me to Lily and disappears into the office, but not before she has glimpsed the picture on his desk, of Dr. Cole with his arm around a beautiful woman who has long red hair—an older version of Bish.

Lily withdraws, closing up inside, and carries me down the hall. On a corkboard on the wall, photos of various dogs and cats are posted next to squares of paper. On the paper are cryptic, scrawled notes. Lily reads aloud:

"'Dr. Cole saved Toby's life. We love him forever.'" Then another one: "'Dr. C, thank you for fixing my kitten.'" She looks at a wooden plaque. "The city honored him for services to various organizations and for volunteer work to help wildlife in the community. Oh, look at these cards from people whose animals have died." There's a picture of a striped tabby cat with green eyes. "'Dr. Ben Cole is a wonderful doctor.'"

She turns and nearly drops me on the floor. "I didn't see you there," she says.

Dr. Cole has been standing behind us. I knew exactly where he was the whole time.

"Sorry I startled you."

"You've touched so many lives." She's impressed, but still all closed up inside.

"Just doing my job." He shoves his hands in the pockets of his lab coat.

"Thanks for saving the cat's life."

"She did it all herself."

"But you helped."

They look at each other, and despite all I have done to bring them together, an invisible wall goes up between them again, each of them trapped in a private darkness.

Chapter Twenty-six

Lily

On the drive back to the cottage, nobody spoke. Lily tried to untangle the myriad emotions coursing through her, like rivers meeting and separating and meeting again. She hugged the cat, who was wrapped in the blanket, and savored her weight, her warmth, her tiny beating heart. Perhaps one of her remaining nine lives had come to the rescue. How many did she have left?

Or maybe Dr. Cole had saved her. He seemed the type to quietly perform miracles without a word. What great feat of heroism had he performed in the surgery suite?

Lily still struggled to reconcile the image of the morose, gruff man she had first met with the way his grateful clients perceived him and the way he'd looked in the photograph—young and happy and smiling, his face ruddy and his eyes bright. Together, he and his wife had looked blissful and deeply, irrevocably bonded, as if their love had been made from stardust and sprinkled over them, casting a spell. Together, they gave off an aura of timeless joy.

At the cottage, Dr. Cole parked at the curb. The cat was purring, seemingly undisturbed by the ride this time. Perhaps it was the box that she hated, the confinement. Lily turned to Dr. Cole and smiled. His face appeared angular in the orange half-light from the street lamp.

"Thank you so much," she said, her voice rough with emotion. "She means so much to me now. I love this little cat. Sounds crazy, I know—"

"No, it doesn't. Sounds reasonable to me."

"Honestly, I don't know what happened, but if you hadn't been around . . . If you hadn't rushed her to the clinic, she could've died."

"Believe me, I didn't do anything. She saved herself."

The cat purred louder, as if concurring. Outside, the rain had stopped, and the evening was calm.

"Whatever you say," Lily said, "but I get to thank you anyway." She leaned over and kissed him lightly on the cheek. He didn't move away.

"You're welcome," he said. He turned toward her, his face close to hers, and for a crazy instant she thought he might kiss her. She slid back across the seat and fumbled with the door handle, her other arm still around the cat.

"I'll get that," he said. "You hold on to the kitty. Don't let her go. We should have brought the carrier—"

"We were in a rush."

A moment later, he was opening her door, and she climbed out and hurried to the porch. She thought of how, only a few weeks earlier, she had tried to shoo the cat out of the shop, and now she held on to the little cat for fear of losing her.

Dr. Cole opened the front door, and inside the shop, she let the cat down on the floor. The fluffy thing shook herself and trotted off, tail in the air, as if nothing unusual had occurred.

Dr. Cole stood just inside the door. "She seem okay?"

"Fine," Lily said. "Amazing. Thanks again."

"Call me anytime, day or night," he said.

"I'll try not to wake you."

He looked at his shoes. "Thanks for the suit. I know it was special to you, to your husband."

The words "your husband" sent her heart plummeting. "I couldn't hold on to it forever," she said.

He nodded, lingering. Outside, the gray sky had taken on a turquoise, twilight glow. What was he waiting for? "About the estate sale," he said.

"Oh, the one I circled in *The Monthly*—"

"I know you aren't planning to go, but Bish is looking forward to it. Her mother and I split up a while back."

"I know. Vanya told me. I'm sorry."

He hesitated, nodded again. "The whole thing has been hard on Bish. I wonder if you wouldn't mind taking her."

So, the hesitation had been leading up to this request. "All right, I'll go, but she should get here by seven, which is early, but I need to get back to open the shop by ten."

"She'll be thrilled. Thank you." He tipped an imaginary hat and headed off to the truck.

Lily stood in the doorway, watching him leave, and she felt oddly inert, stuck in time, like a specimen suspended in a jar.

Chapter Twenty-seven

Lily

Early Saturday morning, Bish stood on the porch in the cold drizzle, bundled in a blue parka, jeans, and zebra-striped boots. Her breath rose in puffs of steam. She was certainly unafraid to stand out in a crowd. Lily admired her individuality, her openness—so different from her father's aloof broodiness. Maybe her mother did the same, dressed in bold colors and had a bold personality, too. If so, then Lily could see what Dr. Cole missed about his ex-wife.

"I'm moving to Hawaii," Bish announced, stamping her

boots on the mat. "I'm so sick of this yucky weather. Coming with me?"

"Hawaii? Today? The cat would get lonely." Lily pulled her robe tightly around her waist and looked up at the shifting shades of pewter sky.

"I heard what happened," Bish said. "Is she——?"

"She's better now."

"Oh, good. You could name her Miracle."

"I'll put that on the list of possibilities."

Bish tapped her Mickey Mouse watch. "So why aren't you ready? All the good stuff will be gone. You wanted me to get here early!"

"I'm sorry. I overslept." Lily had gone a bit crazy, heading out on a long, fast walk the previous afternoon, and now her muscles ached. Maybe she'd needed to burn off the extra adrenaline.

She'd dreamed of Josh. He'd felt real, alive. They were in bed together, and then she had noticed a shadow in the corner, advancing toward her, and she had jolted awake, disoriented and mildly aroused. She had run her hand down her body, her nerve endings raw and sensitive. She could still feel Josh—his presence so strong, she could almost touch him, smell him. Then the room closed in around her, and she was wide awake and utterly alone. Even the cat had gone off to chase shadows.

Nobody but Josh could satisfy this acute yearning, and the knowledge that he was truly gone, that no other man would ever *be* Josh had filled her with desolation. She'd had a difficult time getting back to sleep. But eventually she had fallen into a restless slumber, waking only when she heard the banging on the door.

Now Bish was scowling, looking a little like her father. "Earth to Lily! What is going on with you?"

"Sorry—I'll get ready." Lily looked across the street, her heart sinking. What had Flo done with The Newest Thing? Looked as though a construction crew had arrived to plan an addition in the empty lot next door. There were orange markers and stakes in the gravel.

Bish followed Lily's gaze, and her frown deepened. "What are you looking at?"

"'Expansion coming soon.' I'm reading that sign in the window. She's expanding? She doesn't already have enough space? What's she planning to do, sell her consignment pieces in a separate building?"

Bish stuck out her bottom lip, narrowing her eyes at Lily. "Stop. Looking. Over there."

"Excuse me?"

"Either go over and duke it out, or stop looking over there."

"Excuse me, young lady. I can look at whatever I want."

"But it upsets you. Are you going to make your shop work or give up or what?"

"I'm not closing yet." Lily's shop wasn't failing, exactly. She was beginning to gain momentum, but now she suddenly felt like a swimmer trying to stay afloat in an icy sea.

"Then do what you do," Bish said.

"What do you mean, do what I do?"

Bish lifted her boot and waggled it toward Lily. "Be yourself. Like me."

"You're too wise for your britches." Lily smiled. The vague shape of the sun was beginning to peel away the gray veil of sky. "Keep an eye on the cat while I get dressed. And can you feed her? Cans are in the cabinet next to the sink."

"Whatever, boss."

Twenty minutes later, Lily was driving Bish north in the Toyota toward the forested community of West Harbor. Bish chattered the whole way, about school tests, her best friend's boyfriend, about how her dad wouldn't let her wear a normal dress to the Homecoming dance or let her learn to drive before she turned seventeen. Lily murmured in sympathy, distracted. What had the dark shape been in her dream? It had seemed human—and male in character.

Was someone else lingering in her subconscious mind? Dr. Cole? When she looked over at Bish, she saw only the likeness of her beautiful mother, the woman in the photo on his desk. The woman he loved. She had to stop thinking this way.

They found the estate sale at the end of a wooded cul-de-sac. It was not yet eight o'clock, and already people were filing inside. Lily parked the car, and Bish peered out at the stately wooden farmhouse with a wraparound porch—a vision of serenity in a rolling meadow surrounded by outbuildings, gardens, and tall Douglas firs. A *For Sale* sign was planted in the lawn. Everything looked hazy and grayish through a sprinkling of rain. "So everyone who lived there is dead now?"

"Something like that." Lily touched the ring on her necklace.

A flicker of melancholy crossed Bish's face. "It's like all their memories are going to disappear."

As Lily dropped her keys into her purse, she realized that this was one of the most difficult things about losing Josh—knowing that she was the sole keeper of their shared memories. She was the only one who would remember the time he'd dropped the pizza upside down on the sidewalk, or the time he'd left home with shaving cream on his nose.

"I'm sure the family will keep the most important mementos," she said, forcing a smile.

Bish pulled up her left jacket sleeve to reveal a thin jade

bangle on her wrist. "My mom gave this to me. She wears one, too."

"It's beautiful." Lily wanted to hug Bish, but the girl gave off a *don't touch me* vibe.

"Yeah, right, special." Bish made a face, then let down her sleeve.

"If you ever want to talk about it—"

"Thanks, I don't. Let's go in."

Inside the farmhouse, the scents of cedar and spicy potpourri drifted toward them. In each room they found big pieces of furniture, dishes, and lamps for sale. The clothes were few, and they were either falling apart or musty and stained.

Here and there, old family photographs hinted at the past—a slight, curly-haired young woman and her burly husband in uniform, perhaps about to head off to war. Two small daughters, the daughters growing up, the daughters with their own children. The woman and her husband growing older, laughing, the Eiffel Tower in the background, an ocean, a waterfall. Their memorabilia made Lily's heart heavy with lost possibilities.

Was this all that would be left of her when she died? Furniture, a few vintage clothes, and a collection of old photographs? And the ashes of a cat that would surely die before she did? Now she was sinking into melancholy, too. She had to snap out of it.

"Lily, look at that!" Bish pointed at a glittering blue flapper dress hanging on the side of a wardrobe. "Perfect for the Homecoming dance. Is that dress, like, old? Is it vintage?"

"I believe it's an original flapper dress. Seems to be in mint condition. Pretty rare."

"A flapper dress, I knew it. Totally cool."

"Do you even know what a flapper dress is?"

"It's . . . what that dress is. It flaps. That's why it's a flapper."

Lily laughed. "The word has a complicated history. 'Flapper' referred to the woman who wore the dress. Low waistline, no sleeves—a touch of wildness."

"That's me!"

"Why don't you try it on?" But just as Lily reached out to take the dress, a woman grabbed it right off the hanger. She was tall, angular, and elegant, her blonde hair cut in a bob. Either she hadn't noticed Lily and Bish, or she was ignoring them.

Bish gasped, and Lily took her arm and gently steered her away.

Bish yanked back her arm. "Did you even see that?"

"We should let it go," Lily whispered.

Bish's lips trembled. "But every time I want something—"

"You'll find something better."

"Yeah, whatever." Bish receded into a private world, turning the bracelet around on her wrist. She looked bereft, and Lily realized then that if Bish's mother had gone away, she probably wouldn't return to help her daughter shop for a Homecoming dress. Dr. Cole wouldn't have a clue, either. The poor kid.

The woman with the flapper dress had drifted off across the room. "Wait," Lily whispered to Bish. "Stay here. Give me a minute."

Lily strode toward the woman who held the flapper dress draped over her arm. What did Lily plan to say? She didn't have a clue.

"Lovely dress, isn't it?" she said. *I sound ridiculous*, she thought.

Close up, the woman had a boyish face. "It's an original," she said.

"I hope it holds up. Silk can seem strong, even when it's about to fall apart." Lily made a show of looking at the price tag. "Not bad for a flawed piece. That small hole in the fabric could be from a microscopic parasite similar to clothes moths."

The woman's eyebrows rose. "Moths?"

"The larvae eat the clothing. Silverfish, beetles, roaches, or termites will feed on fabric, too, if there's a food or perspiration stain." It was true.

The woman's nose crinkled. "I didn't know that."

"The seams may have been re-stitched on a commercial machine, using cheap, fragile thread."

"Thanks for letting me know." The woman made as if to return the dress, but then she hesitated. An eternity passed. Bish watched and listened from across the room, and Lily imagined that she might be holding her breath.

The woman draped the dress over her arm again. "I'll take my chances. But thanks for the warning." And with that, she walked out of the room.

Lily and Bish stared at the spot where the woman had stood. She seemed to have sucked all the air out with her. But in that empty space, Lily saw the hint of an idea.

"Don't worry," she told Bish. "I've got a dress that might work for you."

"You do?" Bish's face instantly brightened.

"It's the same color as the flapper dress, but it was originally made as a costume for the lead actor in *Cinderella*."

"A Cinderella dress, really?"

"My husband designed it, but I could alter it. We could

tone it down and make it fit you. We could even make it a bit . . . sexy."

Bish's cheeks flushed, and she looked around guiltily, as if her parents might be nearby. Then she lowered her voice. "You could fix it just for me?"

"I'll try. But I can't guarantee it will work."

Bish glanced at her watch. "I have to go to my piano lesson, but I can try to come by the shop. Maybe tomorrow?"

"Whenever you want."

On the rainy drive back to Fairport, Bish leaned her head against the passenger-side window. When Lily parked in front of her house, a log cabin with a green metal roof on a hill overlooking the water, Bish reached over and hugged Lily. "Thanks for fighting for me, for trying to get that flapper dress."

"I'm sorry I didn't succeed."

"Doesn't matter." Bish pulled away, her face pensive. Then she smiled. "You know a lot about vintage stuff. That's you, the knowledge queen. I have a feeling your shop will be okay."

Lily smiled, her eyes filling. "You're a sweet girl."

"I'm not sweet. Don't ever say that. I'm bad, so bad. Just ask my dad."

"Whatever you say."

"See you *mañana*." Bish got out and rushed up the path to the door. A black cat appeared in the windowsill, looking out through startling green eyes. So this was where Dr. Cole lived, too. Lily hadn't pictured such a lush garden of rhododendrons and lavender and fragrant sweetbox.

As Bish opened the front door, Lily glimpsed a shirtless man in the foyer. A ripple of chest muscle, strong shoulders. Her breath caught. It was Dr. Cole. She recoiled as he waved at her. She waved back, then quickly put the truck in reverse. She backed out of the driveway, racing back to the comfort and safety of her shop.

Chapter Twenty-eight

Kitty

When Lily returns to the shop, she unpacks bags of trinkets she bought at the estate sale. Then she looks through many dresses, talking to me the whole time.

"What do teenagers wear these days?" she asked me. "Don't say little short postage stamp dresses. Bish's dad will kill me."

I follow her around, listening with infinite patience.

"He didn't look like himself," she mutters, choosing a glittering black dress, then putting it back on the hanger.

"Do you think he was exercising? I mean, why would he stand at the door without a shirt on?"

I have no idea what she's talking about, as usual.

She finally settles on a puffy dress, a shiny blue thing with big pleats. My paws itch to climb the fabric. "Perfect," she says, and in the morning, Bish shows up to try on the monstrosity.

"This is my idea for alterations." Lily shows Bish some lines scrawled on paper.

"Nobody else will be wearing anything like this," Bish says with excitement. "They're going to be so impressed."

Lily pulls at the loose fabric at the armpit. "This area could come in quite a bit."

"Maybe make the dress shorter." Bish holds the hem up to her knees. "Like up to my thigh?"

"You don't want it that short."

"Everyone's wearing minis. I can show you on Facebook. And tighter?"

"You need to ask your dad about the length. Not too tight, either."

Bish tucks a strand of hair behind her ear. Somehow, the dress makes her features appear even more delicate, almost breakable. I paw at the hem, squint up at her.

"You're so cute, kitty! She wants it shorter, too."

I just like to get up high. If I could, I would sit on her head.

"I'm not making the dress any shorter," Lily says. "Your dad would kill me. I don't want to get on his bad side." She glances at the male statue.

"All my dad's sides are bad. He doesn't even want me to go to the dance. He wants me to study all the time. He doesn't want me to have any fun."

"I'm sure that's not true. He's protective."

"He's the evil version of Shrek. He's totally an ogre. The first chance I get, I'm leaving. I'm not staying on this island."

"Why not? It's so beautiful."

"And boring." Bish sticks out her bottom lip in an exaggerated pout.

Lily is looking across the street at the construction site. Work has begun to add a new building. Then she turns back to Bish. "Where would you rather live? Are you applying for universities?"

"My dad wants me to. But I'm going to take a year off and travel with my mom. France, Italy, Germany, the Greek Islands."

Yet another young human deluding herself with fantasies.

A strange look crosses Lily's face. "The time away might help you figure out what you want."

"Did you take time off?" Bish looks at Lily in the mirror. "Or did you go straight to college?"

College, university, school, jobs—all meaningless words to me, but humans find them important.

"I went straight to college," Lily says. "I kept working. Then I met Josh. I started running his business, and it all worked out for the best."

"How did you meet him?" Bish fusses with the waist of the dress.

"At City Lights bookstore in San Francisco. I was there with a friend, listening to a poet, and Josh was there, too. We looked at each other, and he made some comment about my necklace. He knew it was vintage Chanel."

What a convoluted way to meet a mate. For my species, the introductions are rather swift, the farewells just as quick.

"So it was love at first sight?"

Lily gets the glazed, faraway look. "I suppose it was."

"You didn't graduate?"

"No, but you will, okay?"

"Why? I want to fall in love."

"You can do both. Take a year off, then go to college and finish and you can fall in love, too."

"The next time my mom comes back, she's taking me with her."

Oh, please, dispense with the wishful thinking.

"When is she coming back?"

"Whenever. How would I know?" Bish sticks out her right foot. I can't help myself—I bat at her white knit sock. "Kitty, no! I need nylons and high heels, maybe like two inches."

"Two inches! Isn't that a bit much? You'll look like a . . ."

"I can walk in heels. My mom taught me how. We used to play dress-up."

"Maybe the heels can be a bit lower."

"This is, like, the best dress ever," Bish says, smiling at herself in the mirror. "But I need pumps."

"You need princess shoes. I'll keep an eye out."

"My mom gave me a pair of princess shoes when I was young," Bish says. I sense hollowness inside her, her gaze distant. What do people look at when they stare off like that?

"You're still young," Lily says.

"But I feel really old."

When Bish goes back into the dressing room, I can hear her heartbeat, struggling to hold off the pain. Then the doctor comes inside, rattling keys, and Lily's heartbeat goes haywire again.

"Dr. Cole!" she says. "Your jacket isn't quite finished yet."

"I came to pick up Bish—"

"She's in the fitting room."

He nods. "And to see if you want to grab dinner sometime."

"Grab dinner?" She steps back, as if some hard object has just hit her.

"Yeah, a bite." He shoves his hands into his pockets.

"Uh—"

"I could show you around the island a bit, maybe next Saturday?"

"Show me around the island?"

Why is she repeating everything he says?

"Hey, if you're too busy—"

"No, no! I'm just—I was thinking about my schedule." She looks past him, across the street again.

"So will Saturday work?"

"Yes, Saturday."

"Great, I'll pick you up around eleven."

She nods, still looking stunned, as Bish emerges from the fitting room in her bright, striped clothes. "Dad! Guess what? Lily just showed me, like, the best dress for the Homecoming dance. It's a Cinderella dress and completely magical. It's, like, the best dress in the history of the entire universe."

Chapter Twenty-nine

Lily

What on earth had she just agreed to do? Go out with Dr. Ben Cole, morose father of Bish, jilted ex-husband forever pining for his lost wife? But Lily knew she had asked for this. She'd invited him to the shop to try on a jacket. She'd invited Bish to wear the Cinderella dress. But he'd been so direct, so clear. Was he attracted to her? Or did he feel sorry for her? Was he merely trying to fill his time? Add another notch to his belt?

She traipsed upstairs, the cat in tow, and checked through her clothes in the dresser drawers. She tried on various shirts, sweaters, pants, and skirts and threw each item into one of two piles on the bed. "Maybe and no," she said, pointing to one, then the other.

The cat climbed onto the Maybe pile, but Lily picked her up and moved her onto the bedspread. She promptly climbed onto the No pile, and Lily gave up on moving her.

"What am I doing?" she asked.

The cat squinted at her.

"I'm a wreck. I don't know how to go on a date. I don't want to go on a date!" She leaned over the dresser and peered at her face in the mirror. A gaunt stranger, with large eyes set a little far apart and crow's-feet, stared back at her with a slightly scared, haunted expression.

"Dammit, Josh, I don't want to go out with other men. Don't make me have to . . . put myself on the market again. Dress up, fix my hair, worry about what I look like to some-one else." She remembered their nights snuggling in front of the television in their pajamas, watching *Masterpiece Mystery*. She and Josh had become so comfortable with each other—there were no secrets or closed doors between them.

"I'll never feel that comfortable again with anyone else. Takes way too long. But here I am, back in dating mode again when I never wanted to be. Ooh, not a date. An out-ing. But dinner. What do you think? I have to do this even-tually, don't I?"

The cat squinted and purred.

"I look terrible. Not terrible. I have bone structure. Don't I?"

More purring.

"I need makeup. It's all old and dusty in these containers." She rummaged in the top drawer, found a container of foundation, then brushed glitter onto her skin. The powder crumbled. "This stuff is too old. How do I look? Will he even notice? Do I even want to do this?" She couldn't imagine going to the cosmetics counter at a department store and trying to find new makeup. She supposed she ought to try to look nice in the shop, as well. Maybe she came across as austere, but she wasn't selling herself. She was selling clothes.

But she did want to look beautiful, didn't she? Even though she could never enter a relationship with Dr. Cole? This would be a casual outing, but still. He'd asked her out for a reason.

She put the makeup back in the drawer and looked at the two piles of clothes. Since when had she stopped caring what she wore, even with a store full of beautiful vintage garments? She could choose something from downstairs. She could and she would.

"I feel like a teenager. Silly and fluttery. What will Josh think of me?" She felt a sudden draft, a breath of cold air and the sensation of darkness. Was Josh here with her? Did he sense her buzz of confusion and excitement? The change inside her?

The cat looked up toward the junction of the wall and ceiling. Lily followed her gaze. "What do you see? Nothing there." If Josh was really here, if he knew about her date, he showed no sign. Nothing moved in the room, and Lily heard no sound except the cat purring and the beating of her own heart.

Chapter Thirty

Saturday morning, Lily put on a mauve turtleneck sweater, jeans, thick socks, and sneakers—nothing fancy for a late-autumn outing on a blustery island with Dr. Cole. She was barely ready when she heard the knocking at the back door.

The cat leaped off the bed and rushed through the kitchen, as if she had been waiting for him. When he stepped into the mudroom, dressed for rain in an all-weather jacket, hiking pants, and waterproof boots, Lily's mind rushed back to the image of him at his front door, shirtless. Could he see what she was thinking now?

He winked at the cat and petted her, then grinned at Lily. "Ready for an island tour?"

"Ready as I'll ever be."

"Let's get one thing straight," he said, frowning at her. *Uh-oh.* "Yes?"

"Stop it with the Dr. Cole stuff. Call me Ben."

"Ben. Okay. I like that name."

"Don't have a choice. It's what I got."

"And Lily's what I got."

"Good name. You're like a flower."

"Thanks." She blushed.

He spoke in a simple, direct way. No candlelight, no romance, but somehow she found that his words affected her.

She grabbed her purse and they pulled up their hoods and ran out through the rain to the truck. He'd tidied up inside. The library book and papers were gone. She found this endearing.

He drove through downtown to a secluded cove that she hadn't known existed, but was close to town and easily accessible by car. The beach was rich with driftwood, rock, shells, and barnacles; the air was scented with sea salt and kelp.

"Bish and I call this our secret beach," he said, "although I'm sure it has a name. I just can't remember what it is."

"Thanks for showing it to me. This is amazing!"

They hiked down a narrow path to a flat stretch of sand. He pointed across the water at a line of distant lights. "Seattle seems so far away, like a mirage."

She shielded her eyes, her hair whipping in the wind. "I didn't think so many boats would be out when the sea is choppy."

"Speedboats are always out, but you don't see many sailboats on a day like this. You always see eagles." He pointed back toward the bluff, where madrone and fir trees leaned over the beach, their gnarled roots clinging to the cliffside. An eagle soared on an updraft, letting out a high-pitched shriek.

"There's a nest over there." Ben pointed to a tall fir. "I've seen four or five eagles circling. There's another one. And another."

Three bald eagles with magnificent wingspans sailed high in the air. Ben and Lily followed them along the beach, picking their way across rocks and shells, barnacles and kelp.

"Watch out," he said as they approached a concrete boat ramp. "You almost stepped on a fish."

Lily looked down and jumped backward. Littering the ramp were several large fish heads, some with spines still attached. Now she could smell them, too. Josh had hated the smell of fish, would've gagged at this stench, but Ben didn't bat a lash. Lily supposed he was accustomed to bad smells in his profession. "This would be heaven for the cat," she said. "Fish everywhere. What happened here?"

"Seals were feasting, I suspect." He pointed to other small carcasses on the sand, then to a round, dark shell with spiny protrusions. "Sea urchin. I rarely see a shell intact."

"They look so fragile."

"In the water, those spikes are good protection. But when they're away from their natural habitat, thrown up on the beach, they're vulnerable."

"I'll try not to step on them."

"Bish used to be scared of them when she was little. She wouldn't even wade into the surf."

Lily imagined Bish as a baby, then as a toddler, and she felt the pain of opportunity lost. The soul of any baby that she and Josh might've had would remain in the primordial soup forever, in the land of what might have been.

"Are you okay?" Ben was looking at her, concern in his eyes.

"I'm fine. I was just thinking, um . . . Bish is an unusual name. She said it wasn't short for anything—"

"But it is. It's short for Bichon Frise."

She couldn't help smiling. "Are you kidding? You

named your daughter after a small breed of fluffy white dog?"

He laughed and shook his head as if he couldn't quite believe it either. "It was Altona's idea. She wanted to name all our kids after dog breeds. We didn't get past one. Can you imagine naming a kid Keeshon, Pug, or Beagle?"

"Or Corgi or Rottweiler?"

"Rotty for short?"

They burst into laughter. "How does Bish feel about it? Let me guess. She tells everyone her full name is Bish, like she told me."

"I asked her if she wanted to officially change her name, but she refused. Maybe she'll change it when she's older. What could I do? I was in love with Altona. I went along with what she wanted."

"I did that with my husband, too, went along with what he wanted. Not that he was domineering. If I wanted something, he was happy to oblige. I just rarely had a preference."

"Did you two plan to have kids?"

"We both wanted one from the start."

"Were you high school sweethearts?"

"I met him in college. How about you and your wife? Ex-wife, I should say."

He hunched his shoulders against the wind. "I met her

in the second grade. We both went to Fairport Elementary. But she was a restless type even then. I knew that about her." A muscle twitched in his jaw. "When she got the job offer of a lifetime, we both knew."

"She chose to travel."

"International Corporate Event Planner. That's her official title now. When her big break came, that was it. She had to go, and I had to stay here, to give Bish stability."

"I'm sorry. That must've been so hard."

"It was the worst thing that's ever happened—well, except for my dad dying and my goldfish going belly up when I was ten." He threw another flat rock into the waves, where it skipped four times before sinking.

"Josh dying was the worst thing that's ever happened to me, bar none."

"I can understand that. If you don't mind my asking, how did he die?"

"Car accident." How easy it was to say two simple words, when the memories came in a broken mosaic of many black moments—the impossibly long drive to the trauma hospital, the eternal wait, the grim-faced doctor leading her past other patients, blood on the floor, and Josh lying so still, so cold, and yet, with the sheet pulled up to his chin, his eyes half-open, he had seemed, at first, to be looking at her. What had happened next? She must've crumpled. Somebody held her up by her armpits. Somebody had brought her water. People were talking to her, but she rested her head on Josh's chest and sobbed. How surreal it had felt not to hear his heartbeat.

"I'm sorry," Ben said.

"Thanks." She couldn't help it—the tears came, and she realized she hadn't let herself cry in months.

"Sorry I brought it up." He handed her a crumpled tissue from his pocket.

"No, it's good, just a little embarrassing."

"Hey, I see people cry all the time at the clinic; well, not all the time. They're happy a lot of the time, too."

She laughed through her tears. "I'm sure they are."

"I've been known to cry now and then myself."

"No, you? Impossible."

"Believe it or not. I cried when Altona left, still cry sometimes, even at little things."

"I still miss the little things about Josh," she said, sniffing into the crumpled tissue. "He used to write notes on scraps of paper. 'Coffee for you, my love,' he would write and put the note next to the coffeemaker. He'd leave one in the bathroom next to my toothbrush. 'Thinking of you.' I kept all the notes in a wooden box. After he died, I took them out and posted them everywhere, in the places he'd left them, like he was still around."

Ben flung another rock into the water, but this one sank. "When Altona packed her bags, I hid one of her sweaters, just an old wool rag that was starting to unravel. She only wore it around the house. I thought she wouldn't miss it. At night, you're not going to believe this, I kept it next to my pillow and sniffed it."

"I kept Josh's shirt under my pillow. I still do, sometimes. I sold many of his things, but I kept a few, the ones that smelled like him. I've got his shoes and shirts in the closet."

"I wanted to smell Altona, too. But then she came back looking for the sweater."

"She came back for it, really?"

"Yeah, and I gave it to her. Pretended it had fallen behind the dryer. Crazy."

"I think we all do crazy things, when we lose someone. At a support group, I met a widow who scrawled notes on blackboards all over the house. She wrote what she was thinking, what it was like to be a widow, to be alone."

"What's it like?" He looked at her with genuine curiosity. She liked this about him, his openness—maybe he and Bish were more alike than she had thought.

What was it like? Nobody had ever asked. Instead, they'd told her what she was supposed to feel or tried to pacify her or given her instructions about the afterlife. "It's like half of me was ripped away. More than half. My heart, all my insides, my limbs."

"I'm sorry. That sucks."

"Yeah, that's a good way to describe it. What about you? What about Bish? It must've sucked for her when her mom left."

"Bish pretends to be a grown-up, to be over it. She knows her mother isn't mom material. Altona knew it, too. But a girl needs her mother."

"She doesn't have any contact with Altona?"

"Hell, Altona forgot to call on her own kid's birthday. She called the next day, said she'd been traveling, didn't get a cell phone signal. Bish chose to believe it. Altona apologized, and Bish pretended to forgive her. What else could she do?"

"The poor kid."

"She likes you, and she loves that dress. Nobody's ever done that for her, sewn a thing to fit her."

"It's my pleasure. But I don't know if I'll do a good job."

"You'll be great."

"Thanks, but the jury is still out."

"No, I mean it. You're great."

"You're not so bad yourself."

They were both quiet, listening to the wind, the surf,

the call of seagulls. How could Bish's mother have abandoned her family? How could she not be involved in her daughter's life?

In the distance, a gaggle of cormorants floated on the waves. The damp, cold air brought Lily back to life, her senses on the alert. The sky darkened, and she and Ben sprinted back to the truck just as the sprinkling rain became a downpour.

"I know another place we can go," Ben said, damp hands on the steering wheel. "A quintessential island destination, and it's indoors."

"All right, if it's indoors, then it qualifies."

He drove along a country road that led past gently rolling hillsides, farmland, and old Victorian farmhouses. The pastoral island, open and airy, allowed Lily's soul to relax and breathe.

He parked the truck on a grassy bluff overlooking the sea. "Rain's stopped for now. We can make another dash for it."

"Where are we going?" she asked as they headed out across a grassy field. A white building emerged from the mist, its wavy glass windows reflecting the silvery light, a white tower rising into the clouds.

"A lighthouse!" she exclaimed.

"I want to show you the tower. You have to go up an iron spiral staircase to get up there, but the view is spectacular."

She nodded, swallowing a dry lump in her throat. As she and Ben jogged through the wet grass and rain, she wanted to climb up into that tower with him, but how could she tell him that she was afraid of heights, that she would freeze up on the second rung of the spiral staircase?

Chapter Thirty-one

"The lighthouse is run by volunteers now," Ben said, slowing to let Lily catch up. "Limited hours, but I know people who work here. I asked a friend to come down and open up the place for us."

"Wow, you had this all planned out?"

"I just made a phone call." He led her up the steps and into the lighthouse, which smelled of old wood and dust. "This was one of the few remaining stucco lighthouses in the northwest. Most new ones were made of concrete. The original was made of wood, but it was torn down a long time ago."

"I didn't even know this was here," Lily said, following him into the main room of the tiny museum. In the center of the room stood an old beacon light encased in glass. "The original beacon is missing," Ben said. "Nobody knows where it is. But this one was used while the sailing ships still came down through the strait, gathering wind for the journey south."

"How does one gather wind? Does the sailboat pick up speed and then drift south on the strength of the air trapped in its sails?"

"Good question—who knows?" He smiled at her. The wind whistled somewhere up in the rafters. "Hello, Dirk?" he called out.

A gray-haired, fresh-faced man, athletic and wrapped in fleece, emerged from a small room with a sign reading *Gift Shop* above the door. "Hey, Ben, good to see you."

The men shook hands. "This is Lily," Ben said. "She's new to the island. I'm showing her around. Makes me see my home through new eyes."

"That it will." Dirk shook Lily's hand, too, his fingers thick and warm, and she felt as if she had just been inducted into a secret society. "You can take him out any day if it gets him to see old friends. You'd think we'd see a lot of each other on an island this size, but I guess Ben has been holed up in the clinic."

"Making a living," Ben said.

"I hear you. We just lost our state funding. Running on volunteers now."

"Man, that bites."

"Yeah, well. It's the state of the world." Dirk waved an arm upward. "Tower's open. Go for it."

"Thanks for opening up the lighthouse for us."

"I got paperwork to take care of anyway. Let me know if you need anything." Dirk headed back into the gift shop, and Ben motioned for Lily to follow him into the hall and up a steep, iron spiral staircase. No turning back now, not when Dirk had obviously come in just to open the tower for them.

Lily's hands were clammy, her heartbeat fast. Ben stepped up ahead, turned, and reached down a hand. "Steep staircase here."

"I can manage." She gripped the railing, not looking down as she climbed each narrow step. How silly it would be to freeze up now. But by the fifth step, she had to sit down.

"Are you all right?" Ben asked.

She looked up at him, her legs rubbery. "I get vertigo."

He came back down and took her hand. "I'll help you."

She tried two more steps, then sat down again. "I'm really sorry. I feel so stupid. It's the steps—I can see right through the rungs and all the way down—"

Before she finished speaking, Ben swept her into his arms in one swift movement, carried her up the last of the stairs, and deposited her, breathless, at the top.

"Whoa!" she said, grabbing the railing in the tower room. "Thanks. I didn't expect that kind of service."

"You okay?" His eyebrows drew together. "You look a bit pale."

"Fine—this is great. Thanks." She hadn't realized he was so strong. She joined him at the window, and a small thrill rushed through her. "Look, you can see across the water. There's a freighter, and a navy ship. What a view."

"The beacon was for the older ships, the ones that ran on sails instead of steam. Not because these waters were treacherous, but to guide them south into the Sound. There are some strong currents along the west side of the island here."

To the left, near the waterfront, a series of square concrete buildings stretched out in rows, like battle fortifications. "What are those?" she asked, pointing. "They look like something out of a science fiction movie."

"Used to be our hidden army base here, a lookout. See that cannon, the black one?"

"That's a real cannon?"

"Used to defend our coastline. Everything's been decommissioned now. Kids like to climb on the old foundations. There are drop-offs and signs reading *Falling Can Be Deadly.*"

"So it can." In more ways than one. She was beginning to shiver, but she felt she could stay up there, standing next to Ben, looking out on the blustery shoreline, forever. "What's that brown lump in the grass?"

"That's one of the island's many rabbits. We had a program to trap and neuter them, but we can never get all of them. That one looks like a wild rabbit, though."

"It's so large."

"They do get big here. Too bad Miss Marmalade isn't here to catch them. She was the lighthouse cat for many years. She kept the ghosts in line, too."

"Ghosts?"

"Word was, the ghosts of sailors lost at sea would follow the beacon inland and haunt the lighthouse. Miss Marmalade scared them away. Something about her orange color."

"Miss Marmalade. I like that name."

He stepped closer to her. Now she could see the stubble on his jaw, the lines on his skin, the bluish tint in his pale gray eyes. She wanted to touch his cheek. She curled her fingers into the palms of her hands, which were safely ensconced in her pockets now.

He took another step, even closer. Was he going to kiss her? If he tried, she thought she might faint. No, he pointed at something past her, out the window to the north. "Just over those hills, there's a great walk along the bluff. It was even featured in *Sunset* magazine. On a better day, I'll show you. And the views are breathtaking." But he was looking at her, not at the view. She could smell his fresh soap, the hint of promise. *On a better day, I'll show you.*

"On a better day, a hike would be great." A different woman spoke, not her—someone who felt hopeful and reckless. Now she could feel his breath on her cheek. Anything could happen, anything at all.

Then he stepped back, away from her, and her heart fell. Could she be disappointed? Did she want him to kiss her, despite everything? Had she been waiting for him to try? But she realized he would not. He wouldn't kiss her because he viewed her as a widow in mourning. Because his own wife had left him and he had not recovered.

"Come on, I have another place to show you," he said, heading back to the staircase to wait for her.

"I can make it down on my own," she said.

"If you're sure." He stopped on the top step with his gloved hand on the railing. For a split second, she pictured him taking off the glove, touching her cheek. She shouldn't imagine such things. They both had enough baggage between them to fill an airport conveyor belt.

"The place I wanted to take you is the graveyard," he said. "It's rich with history, but maybe it's not a place you want to go?"

"I don't mind at all," she said. She wondered if she might see Josh there. Why hadn't she thought of it before? Ghosts were drawn to headstones, weren't they? He didn't have one—no burial place, no particular spot where family could go to remember him. If he'd gone anywhere after she'd seen him standing in the street, it would surely have been the cemetery.

Chapter Thirty-two

The old part of the graveyard sat on a gentle, sloped hill-side surrounded by rolling farmlands. Old Victorian farmsteads still dotted the fields, and beyond the grave-yard, the sea sparkled through the trees, the Olympic Mountains rising jagged and white in the distance. Ben led Lily up the path, past the new section, then veered to a spot where weathered marble headstones rose above the earth, shaded by ancient fir and maple and oak trees.

"This is where you'll find the history of the island," he said, taking her to a well-kept family plot, lush with trees and flowers. He showed her the granite headstones for his grandparents. "I spent summers with them, on their farm," he said. "I always tended to their animals. I wanted to be a large animal vet for a while. I still sometimes help people out, but I migrated to smaller animals."

"So it was always your dream to be a vet."

He nodded. "What was yours?"

"I actually always loved to create things," she said, staring off toward the water. "I dressed up my dolls in little retro-cool outfits. I ripped up Barbie doll clothes and remade them. My friends thought I was crazy. I liked to draw pictures of way-out-there clothes, like from science fiction."

"How did you end up in business?"

"I studied design. But my parents wanted me to be practical. They were immigrants, my mother from India, my dad from Ireland. They met here after they moved to America. They were both trying to make a go of their lives. They saw drawing and design as too whimsical. And then I met Josh and fell in love, and he was so creative—his creativity eclipsed mine."

"But not anymore."

"Not anymore."

"We never know how things are going to turn out."

"Like your wife leaving you?"

"Yeah. She was a planner. She must've been planning her departure for months, but I was blind. I had no idea it was coming. Now you could say I've become cautious."

"I don't blame you." But according to Paige, he hadn't been cautious—he'd gone a little crazy for a while.

He led her to the oldest graves in the cemetery. "Captain Fairport is buried right here," he said, pointing to an Eiffel Tower-shaped headstone.

"Fairport was named after him?" In the biting wind, her nose was going numb. She tightened the string of her hood.

"He was beheaded by a group of Tlingit warriors. They stormed his house and killed him in retaliation for the murder of twenty-seven members of their tribe."

"I knew we had a violent past, but it's hard to imagine." She shivered.

"You're cold." He put an arm around her, drawing her close to him. He felt solid, durable. "Should we go back to the car?"

"No, I'm okay. Really, I want to stay." She didn't care that the wind whipped her face, that her jeans were damp from the rain, her feet soaked and nearly numb inside her running shoes. She nearly forgot that she'd agreed to come here to look for evidence of Josh.

"A U.S. warship had already killed several members of the Tlingit tribe," Ben went on. "They were getting payback. Life seems pretty benign and calm these days compared to what went on back then."

She nodded, her teeth chattering. She was distracted by his nearness, by the warmth she could feel through their jackets. His body felt like a furnace.

He led her to the next set of graves, a marble headstone engraved on two sides with the names of two different children, one who had died at age three, the other at age seven. "They hardly had a chance to live," she said, touching the engraved names. Their short lives suddenly put Josh's life into perspective. At least he'd had a chance to grow up, find his profession, make a mark on the world, and fall in love. At least she'd had a decade with him.

"Times were tough," Ben said. "People died young."

"But not always. Look, there's a woman who died at age ninety-six. Muriel Racer. Is that her real name?"

"And she's buried right next to Swift," Ben said. "Truth is stranger than fiction."

"I wish I had my camera." She shivered again.

Ben ran his hand up and down her arm, pulling her closer. "You're numb. Sorry, this hasn't been much of a date so far."

"This is the most unusual date, but in a good way."

He grinned. "Are you hungry? I want to take you to dinner. I was saving the best part for last."

"Dinner? Where?"

"It's a surprise. I'll take you home first so you can put on some dry clothes, and then we'll go." He pulled her close, his arms around her. She could feel the strength of his heartbeat. But still, he didn't kiss her. He took her hand and led her back to the truck.

Chapter Thirty-three

"One big step." Ben reached out his hand from inside the boat. Lily held her breath and stepped off the dock, more like a leap into his arms. The small motorboat swayed dangerously. In the darkening evening, the rain spit down in a cool mist, but the ocean was, thankfully, calm. But Lily still shivered, her teeth chattering again.

"Best way to see the Puget Sound is from the water," Ben said, handing her an orange life jacket.

"You're right. This is quite a surprise." She followed

him into the tiny forward cabin, unsteady on her feet. "Bish didn't mention a boat."

"She gets deathly seasick, and since Altona left, I don't take the boat out much anymore."

The name, Altona, put a damper on the evening, but what did Lily expect? She was conscious of Josh looking over her shoulder at every juncture.

"Sure you know what you're doing? What if we capsize?" she said, only half-joking.

Ben winked at her, his face suddenly handsome in the harbor light. "If we do, I'll rescue you. Promise. I got my life-saving credentials. Seriously, though, I've been doing this all my life. First on my dad's catamarans, sailboats, speedboats, you name it."

"I'm reassured." She sat on a hard plastic bench while he turned on the motor and steered the boat out of the harbor. The noise seared her eardrums as they picked up speed, crashing and bumping through the waves. The wind whipped her face.

Ben kept talking to her as he steered the boat away from shore, but she only pretended to understand his words, which were lost in the noise. She nodded now and then as he pointed toward the forested shoreline. Even though he wore a puffy parka, she could make out the contours of muscle, his broad shoulders.

". . . depth finder," he said, pointing to a gauge on the control panel. ". . . shallow spots . . . have to know your way around."

The farther they traveled from shore, the freer she felt. It was good to be out on the water, the boat pounding across the waves, rattling her bones. She felt fully alive, and the roar of the engine drowned out her fears, her memories. Ben's deep, rumbling voice, and his gloved hand pointing out various features of the shoreline, exhilarated her.

She moved up close to him, and he looked at her and smiled in surprise. "You're cute in that life jacket," he said, putting an arm around her.

Had he just called her cute?

"I look like an orange gorilla," she said.

"You could never look like a gorilla. You're way too pretty." He kept his left arm on the steering wheel, his right arm around her.

When was the last time she'd felt pretty? "So are you," she said. "Not pretty, I mean. Handsome." She had just complimented Ben. No turning back.

He grinned and winked at her, surprising her again. She hadn't thought him capable of winking. She was glad he couldn't see her blushing in the semi-darkness.

"Where are we going?" she said.

"Like I said, it's a surprise." He gave her a look that

suggested all kinds of things, and she smiled and shook her head. Men were unabashed about the pure pleasures—food and adventure and sex. When had she lost her own love for life?

She hadn't thought much about food for a long time. Now the cold night air, all the exercise she'd been getting, and being close to him, made her more than hungry. She was famished. She turned her face into the wind as he maneuvered the boat through the Sound. The lights of Fairport faded behind them.

Soon he cut the engine, navigating the boat into a narrow harbor. Lily could see lights winking on a hill above the shoreline. "What's this place? Is this still Shelter Island?"

"This is West Harbor," he said.

"It's neat to see it from this angle."

"Best restaurant on the island is here, but it takes a long time to get up there if you drive."

"Really?"

"Okay, no, but it's more romantic to take the boat."

"Yes, it is." His efforts to be romantic were endearing as well. She hadn't expected it.

He maneuvered the boat against the dock, moored it there, and helped her out. Then he led her along the dock and up into town. West Harbor felt different from Fairport—new and modern. She looked into boutique and restaurant windows as they walked. In a few pubs, youngsters drank beer and laughed.

"Just one more block," he said, taking her arm. He led her into a crowded restaurant, West Harbor Seafood, overlooking the water. The lights were dim, the atmosphere casual but homey. But in the entryway, they were jostled by the crowd that spilled out onto the sidewalk.

"I had no idea about this place," she said. "Where do all these people come from?"

"Best-kept secret," he said, close to her because of the crowd. "They probably sailed in from the city." His breath smelled minty and fresh. Everything about him was fresh and inviting. Even his pale gray eyes.

"But how will we ever get a table?" she said. "The hostess just told those people—"

"We have a reservation," he said, taking her hand. He led her through the crowd to the counter. "Ben Cole, reservation for two," he said.

The hostess smiled at him and grabbed two menus. "Right this way."

They followed her to a small table by the window. They were away from the crowd, and their table had a lit candle on the tablecloth. Warm air flowed gently from a heating vent in the ceiling. Outside, the sky had cleared, the moon throwing pools of mottled white light across the ocean.

"Enjoy." The waitress handed them the menus and walked away.

"This is beautiful," Lily said, sitting across from him. "Absolutely perfect."

"I'm glad you like it."

"I do." She wondered how many other women he had brought here, how many times he'd come here with Altona. She imagined sitting here across from Josh. He would've appreciated the ambience, the view, the menu. He had been very sensual. She had to stop thinking of him. She grabbed her purse. "If you'll excuse me for a minute."

Ben nodded, and she hurried to the restroom, an expansive lounge with brass fixtures and soft elevator music piped in through invisible speakers. She took a deep breath, gathering her wits.

She expected to look disheveled in the mirror, but she looked . . . pretty. Had some of the gray hair disappeared? How could that have happened? Did her skin look younger? Or maybe it was the lighting in here.

She ran the brush through her tangled locks, wiped away the smudged liner beneath her eyes, and touched up her lipstick. A woman came into the restroom—Paige.

Paige stopped, and her eyes widened. "Lily, fancy meeting you here. Small world!"

"Sure is!" Lily said. "How are you?" Had Paige seen her come in with Ben?

Paige came up beside Lily, shoulder to shoulder, and looked in the mirror. "You on a date?"

"Sort of—"

"This is the best restaurant on the island. Best-kept secret. Now you know!"

"So I hear."

"Who are you with? Ben Cole?"

Lily looked at Paige in the mirror and blushed.

"I was right!"

"It's not serious." Lily fussed with her hair. She was beginning to think a small island could be too small.

"Enjoy the not serious." Paige winked in the mirror.

"He was showing me around the island."

"Showing you, huh?" Paige lowered her voice to a whisper. "Let me know how he is. You know—"

"I'm not going to sleep with him!"

"Uh-huh." Paige winked at her again.

Lily elbowed her. "And who are you here with, my dear?"

Paige's face turned a mild shade of pink. "A guy I met. Not a big deal."

"Spill!"

"At John's wedding. That dress, Lily—"

"You met a guy at your ex-husband's wedding?"

Paige waved her hand. "It's all so new. Very casual right now."

"Keep me posted," Lily said.

"I will!" Paige went into the stall, and Lily hurried out of the restroom and back to her table and fumbled with the menu.

"This is going to sound strange, but I don't know how to do this, how to act on a dinner date," she said. "I haven't been with another man in a while—"

"Neither have I. With another woman, I mean."

She laughed, not believing him. "I don't even know what to order."

"Whatever you feel like having."

She sipped her water. "A luxury. It's been so long since I enjoyed food."

"Close your eyes and choose something."

"Really?"

"Why not?"

She closed her eyes and pointed, but she had to try again, as her first option was prawn and garlic butter pasta, and she was vegetarian. Next was the garden burger. "That's it," she said.

"Pretty tame, but okay." He chose the wild salmon.

She kept an eye out for Paige but didn't see her. She was probably on the other side of the restaurant, out of view.

As they ate their meals and sipped wine, they talked about their histories, their hobbies, the island. Ben had grown up here, his father an attorney who worked in the city and liked to sail in his free time, his mother a teacher. He had two older brothers, one an air force pilot, the other a businessman in Montana.

Ben told her stories from his life, from the clinic.

"Once a pet psychic called one of my clients to tell her that her cat wanted her to leave, that she shouldn't have the cat. What was I supposed to say?"

"You didn't let her get rid of the cat, did you?"

"I told her the psychic was wrong. She could not, under any circumstances, abandon her cat when so many millions of cats are homeless."

"That's what I like about you. You stand up for what you believe in."

"I also have to understand my clients and not judge them."

"You judged me when I first brought the cat in there."

"Sorry if I came across as harsh."

"I know you're a softy."

"I am, huh? Here's to softies." He grinned, and they raised their glasses in a toast.

After dinner, they walked on a stretch of quiet beach where the waves lapped the shoreline in a rhythmic lullaby. Lily felt warm and comfortable walking with his arm around her. In a protected cove, he pulled her smoothly into his arms and kissed her. His lips were warm, firm, and confident. She felt her body coming alive again, unfettered.

"My place?" he said, his voice husky. "Bish is away for the night."

"Yes," she whispered back without a second thought. She'd expected to be careful, to keep her boundaries intact, but at his house, she found herself walking inside with him, letting him undress her and carry her into a land of enchantment. He paid attention to parts of her body, to nerve endings that she'd forgotten even existed, and for a while, she also forgot about Josh.

Chapter Thirty-four

Kitty

Lily returns late, when the moon is high, and she smells of the sea, of Dr. Cole, of bliss and sleepiness. She talks to me while she brushes her teeth and wipes the paint off her face.

"I could have stayed over there but it didn't feel right. I mean, it did feel right, but I couldn't."

Why can't she make up her mind?

She blinks at her reflection in the bathroom mirror. "But was that me? Or someone else?"

Is this really a question?

"I'm still alive. Oh, kitty. I know this sounds crazy—but for the first time since Josh died, I feel like I might survive."

To me, everything a human says can sound borderline crazy. "I don't think I've truly believed that I could ever really live again. I mean, feel things like a touch, the taste of food. But I can."

Of course she can. She's putting on a nightgown, climbing into bed, and pulling me close. In a moment, she is asleep, but the next day, she is different, changed again in a small way. Perhaps she is closer to the woman she once was. Her heartbeat has shifted—a subtle alteration.

She's happy for the next few days, occasionally going out to see Ben, preening beforehand, throwing clothes around before choosing each outfit.

Bish comes in, too, to talk about boys and school and new shoes and other boring subjects, but she's always good to me, bringing me treats.

But Lily's perfume, I can do without. That dusty little bottle that sat on her dressing table for so long? She wiped it off and spritzes her neck with that horrendous, sharp scent. Why doesn't she rely on pheromones? She probably can't even smell them.

When Paige returns to the shop, Lily alters another dress for her, this one a deep red with scratchable lace.

The thin woman with the thin little son comes back in, too, and he reads to me again from a giant picture book. This time, I don't fall asleep. The story is about a naughty cat that runs away from home to join a gang, but then the cat misses his human, calls home from a telephone booth, and meows at the top of his lungs. His human races over in the car to pick him up, and he goes home to live happily ever after. A good story, except what is a telephone booth?

Lily's shop attracts more interesting customers, like a weird guy who unloads pockets full of sunglasses, all of which he removed from corpses at an Arizona funeral home. And a frail woman brings in a zippered green dress. She insists it's over a hundred years old, but Lily explains that plastic zippers weren't used on clothing until the sixties. The woman stalks out in a huff.

The people in the shop keep me entertained, and I entertain them in return, but often I sit in the windowsill, my thoughts drifting to the life I had outside. Occasionally, I wish for a little air, but the feeling quickly passes.

Construction continues on the shop across the street, and one afternoon, the tall woman, who sometimes works on the window displays, comes striding up the path and right into Lily's boutique.

Chapter Thirty-five

"I've wanted to stop in here for a long time," Florence said, unbuttoning her Burberry coat. Her voice came out toffee-smooth and deep, and she looked immaculate. The blustery walk across the street had not displaced a single hair on her well-coiffed head. But close up, she looked older than she had appeared from a distance—her face lined, the skin fragile, her eyes tired.

"I'm glad you stopped by." Lily decided to be polite and

friendly. She wouldn't stoop to petty competitiveness, and yet she stole glances at her window display, her sale racks, and her customers. She counted five women in the shop. How many were in Flo's boutique?

"I heard all about the kitty." Flo strode over to the cat, who sat sphinxlike on a table of scarves, and gently patted her head. "She's adorable."

"But I thought you might not like cats."

"Did Chris tell you that? I love cats. She's the one who doesn't like animals. She's my sister's kid and, well, my sister invested heavily in my business." Flo seemed about to add something more, perhaps to say *That's why I hired Chris, not because she's great at her job,* but she pursed her lips.

"I didn't realize," Lily said. "If you ever want to pet the cat, please feel free. Come in anytime."

"You've got some absolutely lovely pieces." Flo strode to a blue floral Hawaiian dress. "This is Alfred Shaheen?"

Lily nodded, surprised. "How did you know?"

"I love vintage Hawaiian, but I've never trusted myself to know which clothes will sell and which aren't worth their salt."

"Really? I'm not always sure, either. It's hit and miss."

"Like anything, right? I should take more risks with my inventory, but . . . the economy is so fragile these days."

"I can relate to that. But I see you're offering clothes on consignment now."

"I've got to ride the waves of the future," Flo said, coming up to the counter. "But I never know what I'm doing."

"I don't, either," Lily said.

"Still, we keep moving forward."

"We do."

Flo shook Lily's hand. Her bejeweled fingers were long, cool, and firm. "This was a long time coming, honey. I should've met you long ago, but the truth is, I've envied you."

"You've envied me?"

Flo waved her hand. "Oh, you know, the whole quaint cottage look, the little vintage sign in the yard, all the bells and whistles, and I'm stuck in a square brick building right on the sidewalk."

"But you have customers traipsing in and out all the time, and the addition—"

"The addition wasn't my idea. It was my landlord's. He might be preparing to kick me out and move one of his other businesses into the space. But right now, it's all going up under the pretense of helping me out and letting me expand."

Flo had a landlord? "That's not a nice thing for him to do," Lily said.

"Maybe I can talk some sense into him. I'm good at

talking people into things. But I came to ask you something a little crazy."

"What do you mean?" Lily imagined that Flo would ask her to close up shop and leave, or—

"Do you want to join forces? I don't mean literally. But we could coordinate our advertising, have our sales together—it could bring in double the business. I'll send people your way, you send people mine. I could carry a few of your things, you carry a few of mine?"

Lily gaped, at a loss. She had expected Flo to come in exuding swagger and confidence, but not this. "It's an idea," she said slowly. "But you're not around too often."

Flo looked at her fingers, which had begun to tremble. "I've been a caregiver for my mom in hospice. But . . . she hasn't got much time left." She looked up at Lily, her eyes dark with sadness and resignation. "When she's gone, which will be very soon, I expect I'll have more time again."

"I'm so sorry," Lily said, her throat dry. She looked around at her shop, at the care she had taken to arrange the lighting, the mannequins, the displays, all to rival the beauty of The Newest Thing. All this time, she'd had no idea what was really going on. "Why don't you stay for a while, and we can talk? I've got some herbal teas, and there's a soft chair over there in the corner. You could take a break and put your feet up on the ottoman."

The immaculate Florence smiled and shrugged off her coat. "I would love some tea, chamomile or lemon would be fine. And I take a little honey, too, a spoonful if you've got some."

Chapter Thirty-six

Kitty

Lily and Flo have become buddies now. If Flo isn't rushing over here with something to say or something to bring, Lily is racing over to the other shop. Flo sends her customers to Lily for alterations. Lily sends people to The Newest Thing. Many more people come in to see "the cat," and I have to groom my fur far too often, what with all the petting.

I play my dutiful role, pawing at the appropriate dress or suit or vintage wedding gown. People gasp and say I'm an enchanted cat, able to see into their souls and show them what they need. That much is true, since I'm descended from the ancient Egyptian cat goddess, Bastet.

I can also see what Lily might face when she finishes altering the Homecoming dress. She slips the blue Cinderella gown into a garment bag.

"All done," she says to me. "Bish is going to love this new look. What do you think?"

I sit upright and stare at Lily, trying to tell her what I know is coming. But she turns around and leaves the shop. What else can I do? I sit in the window and watch her truck disappear around the bend. Sometimes, humans must discover the truth for themselves.

Chapter Thirty-seven

Lily

Lily had transformed the Cinderella costume into a one-shoulder A-line evening dress in royal blue. With each step, Bish would reveal one tantalizing leg, and yet the hem nearly reached the floor, keeping it formal. Lily had sewn ruffled flowers along the bodice and up over the shoulder strap, and as a final touch, she had added a flowing sash. Simple, yet elegant.

She zipped the dress into a garment bag and tried to keep to the speed limit on the drive through town. What would Ben say when he saw her? He'd called her the morning after their night together. He said he missed her, wanted to see her again, only he wasn't sure when he could get another day off. Now she was full of anticipation, checking her face in the mirror, her hair.

When she arrived at the Cole house, Ben's truck was gone, and an unfamiliar silver Mercedes Impressor sat in its place, nose against the garage. Before Lily turned into the driveway, she already knew to whom the car must belong. She could keep on going, drive right into the ocean, but instead she parked behind the Mercedes, draped the garment bag over her shoulder, and strode up to the front door. *Head high, shoulders square. Deep breath, nothing to worry about,* she thought. Maybe Ben had bought a new car. The Mercedes could be his or it could belong to anyone—a friend, a client.

No, there was no way around it. The car belonged to Altona. Maybe it would be best to go home, stop by after Altona had gone, but Lily rang the doorbell and waited. Her nose was cold. The sun peered out from behind a wispy cloud, stark rays reaching across the rooftops at a sharp angle. A dry wind blew dead pine needles across the mossy lawn. What was she doing here? She already felt like an intruder.

The muffled thud of footsteps approached in the hall. The door opened a couple of inches, revealing a woman's large blue eye and curly dark lashes. Lily hadn't expected Altona to answer the door.

"Can I help you?" she said in a mellifluous voice, opening the door a little more. Her lips were full and red. She stood a couple of inches taller than Lily, and she emitted the scents of baby powder and lavender.

Don't be a coward. "I'm here to see Bish."

"You must be Lily." The door opened all the way, and Altona stepped back into the foyer and smiled. Her hair tumbled past her shoulders in a cascade of rich mahogany. She wore one of Ben's plaid flannel shirts—white and pale blue to match her eyes. The shirt extended down to her thighs, revealing bare, Barbie doll–perfect legs that ended in shapely bare feet. Her toenails were painted sparkling pink. Close up, Lily could see a smattering of delicate freckles everywhere on her skin—on her neck, forearms, thighs, nose. The shirt was buttoned to just above her breasts. Somewhere in another room, a clock ticked, and Lily smelled frying eggs and heard faint classical music playing on a stereo—Bach's Brandenburg Concerto, but she couldn't recall which one. And she heard the tumble and click of clothes in a washing machine.

"Is Bish here?" She felt suddenly like a vampire waiting for an invitation across the threshold.

"They'll be back soon. Come on in. I have to get back

to the eggs." Altona held the door open with one hand, a spatula in the other.

"I should come back later."

"Why don't you come in and wait? Bish said you might stop by this morning."

"Might? I told her I would for sure. But really, I don't want to disturb you—"

"You're not disturbing anything."

Lily stepped inside, somehow frumpy and diminished in her running shoes, slacks, and sweater, although Altona was not even dressed. She reached past Lily to close the door.

"Maybe if you just tell Bish—"

"Then they had to stop by the clinic. Ben had an emergency, as usual." Her voice ended on a bitter note.

"I understand."

"Follow me. You can wait in the kitchen." Altona was already gliding back down the hall, beckoning Lily with the spatula. Lily watched Altona's calf muscles moving, a slight swing in her hips.

"Smells good," Lily said in the spacious kitchen. She tried to sound cheery.

Altona rushed to the iron pan on the stove and flipped the omelet. "The key to a good omelet is to whip the eggs well before you pour them into the pan. Mince the garlic and then chop the onions into small pieces."

"You must be a professional." Lily stood awkwardly, the dress still over her shoulder.

"I'm far from professional. I only cook when I'm home." A gold band flashed on Altona's ring finger. Was this really happening? Were she and Ben together again? Had she moved back into the house? "Oh, I'm rude. Would you like some coffee, tea?"

"I'm fine." All the joints in Lily's body felt as though they were dissolving.

"So you made a Homecoming dress for Bish," Altona said. "That was nice of you."

"She wanted a flapper dress that we found at an estate sale, but somebody else got to it first. Bish was disappointed. So I promised to find another dress for her."

"She didn't tell me that." Altona stopped flipping, held the spatula suspended for a split second, then lifted the frying pan and slid the omelet onto a plate.

"I'm sure she planned to tell you."

"She tends to omit things. Oh, the eggs will be cold by the time they get back. Typical."

Typical? Was it typical for a mother to abandon her daughter and then return months later and act as if she'd never left? "I should go. Maybe Bish can come by the boutique, and I'll—"

"Why don't you show me the dress?" She turned off the stove, washed her hands.

"Right now? Here?"

"Go ahead. I'm dying to see it."

Lily unzipped the garment bag and carefully extracted the dress. Altona caught her breath. "Oh, my, that's lovely. The perfect color for Bish."

"I want to make sure it fits. I made a bunch of changes."

"It's a good length, but the slit on the side—"

"It doesn't reveal much." Lily glanced at Altona's bare legs. "The alternative was a very short dress."

"Oh, I know, the girls are wearing mini-skirts this year."

"Exactly, and I thought this would be a little more elegant."

"It's gorgeous."

"Thank you. My husband made it, originally."

"I heard he passed away. I'm sorry." She didn't sound surprised. Had Ben told her? What else had he told her? "You picked the right dress for Bish. Reminds me of something I want to show you—follow me."

She led Lily deeper into the house, toward the master bedroom. They passed Bish's room, the door open. The black cat lay asleep on a plush comforter, and Lily caught a quick impression of a busy teenager's bedroom: posters of heartthrobs on the wall, including a big-haired boy who played a vampire in a wildly popular movie; books and a computer on the desk; a few ribbons and trophies; clothes and shoes strewn about.

"I didn't take the photo albums when I left," Altona said. She opened a closet at the end of the hall. On the top shelves were folded linens; on the bottom were photo albums. She ran her fingers along the spines, pulled out a red album. "Come and see."

Lily went over and stood next to her. The photos were arranged in chronological order: Bish as a baby, with a young, handsome Ben holding her, smiling down at his swaddled baby; the three of them together in the yard; Bish on a swing set; Bish in a bubble bath; Ben pushing her on a bicycle with training wheels. It was the story of a family, which showed Bish getting older, her hair getting longer, and finally there was a picture of Bish in a beautiful, shiny blue dress.

"Graduation from middle school," Altona said. "More of a little girl dress, but it's the same blue. It was always her favorite color. Now she doesn't fit into that dress anymore."

"She looked so beautiful."

"Yes, she did." Altona shut the photo album and put it back in the closet. Then she stood and looked at Lily. "She gets more beautiful as she gets older."

"She certainly does. Well, I should be going." The air had become oppressive, full of the memories of a family in which Lily did not belong. "Bish can try on the dress later—"

"Maybe tomorrow? I'm taking Bish shopping today," Altona said, following Lily back down the hall.

Lily went back to the kitchen for the dress. "She can call me."

"Do you talk to her a lot? I mean, does Bish tell you things?"

"Excuse me? Depends what you mean by *things*."

"About boys she likes, what she's up to at school? That kind of thing?"

Lily shook her head. "She probably prefers to talk to her friends."

"Does she talk about me?"

"Just that she misses you." This wasn't a lie, exactly. Bish had shown Lily the jade bangle. Altona supposedly wore a matching one, but Lily didn't see it on her wrist.

"I miss her so much, too. Sometimes you have to get away from a situation to realize that you miss it."

"I suppose so," Lily replied. How could she make a graceful escape?

"I had to go clear to Hong Kong to realize how much I missed this little island. It's so serene, quiet. The birds, the clean air."

"It is a beautiful island." *Oh, Lord, give me the strength to walk out of here.*

"And this house. I got so sick of it, you know?" Altona pressed her hands to her temples. "I felt like I was going to explode."

"I can understand that. Sometimes we need a change of scenery."

Altona rubbed her temples now. "But it wasn't just that. It was family. My family. There are the little things that you miss. Breakfast, for example." She gestured toward the cooling eggs on the countertop. "I have many things to work out, regrets. But who knows if we can go back in time?"

"I've wondered the same thing myself." Lily's voice wavered. Now she knew, for sure, that she couldn't take this route forward, no matter what. "Look, um, I really need to get back to my shop."

Altona stood. "Of course. I'll let Bish know you came by with that beautiful dress. I'm sure we won't find a better one."

Lily was already heading for the door, but she stopped and turned around. "A better one?"

Altona ran her hand down the front of Ben's shirt, over her flat belly. "For the Homecoming dance. I told her I would buy her one at Nordstrom. A perfect Homecoming dress. I owe her that much. Lace, chiffon, matching pumps, tiara, corsage. The works."

"The works." A sour taste filled Lily's mouth.

"But you've already made her such a beautiful dress. I can't imagine why she would want anything else. Why would she?"

"Yes, why would she?" Then Lily was out the door, gunning the engine out of the driveway so fast, she nearly crashed into Ben's approaching truck in her haste to escape.

Chapter Thirty-eight

Kitty

Lily returns to the shop in a whirlwind, still carrying Bish's blue dress in the bag. Did Bish not like the thing? I don't blame her. Clothes never appealed to me. I'd be happy to turn the gown into a warm bed. Lily takes the dress out of the bag, brandishes the scissors, and almost cuts into the hem, but then she seems to change her mind and tucks the scissors back into the drawer.

"Stupid, stupid, stupid. Why did I think I could fix a dress for Bish? Why did I think Altona would never come back? Why should it matter?"

What is she going on about? What happened out there? Must've been worse than I expected.

She puts that clock sign on the front door, the one that indicates she'll be back later. But she doesn't leave. I follow her upstairs, where she wipes the makeup off her face, including the black smudges under her eyes. I push my head against her to comfort her, and she pets me absent-mindedly. Then she goes to the closet and brings out a box. I recognize what she's taking from inside—they're called photo albums. Lily is turning the pages, telling me about the pictures, so I pretend to look at them and try not to yawn.

That must be her mate, the one whose spirit flits around in the shop. In the photos, he's easy on the eyes, for a human.

"Here we are up at Mount Rainier," she says, pointing to a picture of her and the man, with a bunch of white stuff in the background and a few trees. They're both smiling, their noses red. Her nose is red now, too, from crying. "Here we are at a theater fundraiser."

And on and on. She ignores her cell phone, which keeps ringing. Not like her to ignore a call. Not like her to ignore the regular shop phone, either. Finally there's a banging on the door, and we both go downstairs to answer the door. The doctor comes in, running his fingers through his hair. He forgot to put on a jacket—his shirt and pants are damp.

"Sorry we weren't home when you got there," he says to Lily. Why is he out of breath? He parked crooked at the curb, not a good sign.

"Don't worry about it," Lily says, but her tone says the opposite.

"I had an emergency at the clinic, dog with road rash. A poodle was riding in the bed of the truck, no carrier—"

"Oh, I hope the poor thing will be all right." Lily is standing back, away from the doctor, her arms crossed over her chest in a protective stance.

I wonder if the dog was Fifi?

"It was serious but I think the little guy will survive."

"I'm glad. Where's Bish? Did she come with you?" Lily glances toward the window. The addition is going up quickly on the shop across the street.

Ben looks at the table on which Lily has laid the dress. "I thought I should come on my own, so you and I can talk."

"About what?" Her voice is clipped, her heartbeat sad.

"About Altona being at the house. That shouldn't have happened. You finding her there. I'm sorry."

Uh-oh. The ex-wife was at the house? So that's the unfamiliar scent on his skin.

"I'm glad she was there, in a way. I should get my head out of the sand." But Lily is gazing out the window, not pushing her head into any sand.

Ben takes a step toward her, and she takes a step back. "All I can say is I'm sorry."

"You don't have to explain. Honestly, it's not my business."

"Altona and I—we have a history."

Lily tightens her arms across her chest, as if this will make a stronger shield. "This is your family, your life. I've got a history, too. Unfortunately, my husband is no longer here. I can't test things out to see if it might still work between us."

Ben's face has gone pale. He presses a hand to his forehead. "I didn't mean for it to happen. But she came back."

"It's okay. You don't have to explain to me."

"I feel a need to, for some reason. I don't want to hurt you."

She looks at the mannequin that is now wearing a new suit, since Lily gave the old jacket to Ben. A small, derisive laugh comes out of her. "You think you're capable of hurting me more than I've already been hurt? Who do you think you are?"

"You're right. I know. Believe me, I do. Be angry with me, but I hope you'll still give the dress to Bish."

Lily looks at the dress. "I was going to cut it to pieces. But then I looked at it and I thought, it's beautiful. I can't destroy it."

"Don't ruin it. Bish will love it."

"Her mom should get her a dress. Altona said she was taking Bish shopping today. She showed me a picture of the three of you on a ski lift at Tahoe and—"

"She did what?"

"It's okay—you two were married. You have photos."

"I'm sorry she did that, but I can't erase my past. I can't let everything go and pretend it didn't happen."

"Neither can I."

"No, you can't. Your husband will always be with you. You wear him around your neck. How can I ever compete with a dead man?"

Lily's hand flies to the vial on her necklace. Her face is ashen now. She says nothing, and Ben looks regretful. They stare at each other for a moment, and when he walks out the door, there is nothing I can do.

Chapter Thirty-nine

Lily lay in bed in the early morning, during the hazy moments between sleep and waking when anything still seemed possible, when Josh could still be lying beside her. He could get up and yawn and run water in the bathroom, his hair tousled. She could wake up and smile at him, find his things on the bureau—pennies and crumpled dollar bills and a stick of gum. He could get dressed, stuff his things back into his pockets, put on his watch. Make a pot of coffee. They could make plans for the day.

She held on to a dream of him, but this time, he'd

appeared only as a vague essence. She could not conjure a clear image of his face, and as the gray dawn pulled her into consciousness, he dissipated, and the real world flooded in.

The bureau was as she had left it the night before—messy with junk mail, library books, a pair of socks, a bra. She faced another rainy autumn day alone in Fairport, another day that Ben might be spending with Altona only a few blocks away. Bish might be there, too, sharing breakfast with her parents. Lily imagined them laughing together over cereal or eggs, Ben kissing Altona good-bye. Altona in his long plaid shirt, maybe a different one today—red instead of blue.

Stop it, you can't keep torturing yourself, Lily thought, sitting up. She couldn't let her mind drift to the night she had spent with Ben. In those hours, she had forgotten Josh. Now the universe had decided to punish her. She'd betrayed him.

Dammit, Josh. Come back. She rubbed her eyes. She was crying again, as if Josh had died only the day before. The stages of grief were hogwash. She could ping-pong back and forth from the depths of anguish to moments of joy, and she never knew which one was coming. She hadn't known what she would find at Ben's house, either.

How long had it been since she'd gone over there with the Homecoming dress? A week? Ten days? The hours and days blended together. Had the Homecoming dance already passed? No, it was coming up the following weekend. Bish had not stopped by the shop, but why should she? Altona had probably bought her a perfect dress.

Ben had called a few times, had left messages, but Lily had not returned his calls. What was there to say? She had gone through the motions of life, of running the shop—working with Florence to plan the Winter Downtown Sale; altering more clothes; going to a couple of estate sales on her own; working on her displays.

The kitty stayed with her, a comforting companion, but even the cat could not hold off the night—the soft, quiet hours in which Lily felt particularly alone and vulnerable. How would she move forward? How could she stay in Fairport? She didn't want to run away. In many ways, she'd grown to love the cottage and the town. She knew the checkout clerks at the organic grocery store, the postman, the librarian, the volunteers at the Renewal Society and the Historical Museum. She'd walked the beaches and forest trails. She even liked the tap of rain on the roof, the way the light slanted in through beveled glass windows. She'd come to know which planks creaked in the wooden floor, the particular hiss from the heating vents.

The cat lay across the foot of the bed, grooming her face. She squinted at Lily and purred. If only life could be so simple—eat, sleep, groom, play, purr. Could Lily return to enjoying the simple things? She no longer ate a breakfast of toast and Market Spice tea. She enjoyed a latte now and then from the Java Hut, where she'd gotten to know the tattooed barista. She varied her diet from oatmeal one day to peanut butter the next, maybe a muffin, maybe eggs. In the evenings, sometimes she even cooked. But still, the emptiness persisted.

She hadn't been in love with Ben after all, had she? So she had slept with him. So what? Why did she keep thinking about him? About his pale gray eyes, the way he smiled when he talked about Bish? The way he looked—handsome and determined—when he steered a boat?

He'd been correct in saying that she could never let go of Josh. So how could she fault Ben for holding on to his ex-wife? Was Altona planning to stay with him forever? Would they be remarried?

As Lily got up and moved through her morning rituals of feeding the cat, reading the newspaper, and making her tea, she wondered if she had, in fact, been attracted to Ben from the beginning. He'd been so gentle with the little cat, concerned with her welfare and irritated with Lily, believing she didn't care. Had he been interested in her then, too? Annoyed by his attraction to her? Was that why he'd come over in the night on a house call?

She couldn't know, couldn't gain any perspective. She'd tried to get away. The day after she'd gone over to Ben's place, she'd taken the ferry into Seattle, but the crowds and traffic and high-rises had overwhelmed her—culture shock after her many months on the island. She'd driven north toward Green Lake, where Drew Galt had opened her shop on a pretty, fir-lined street. Drew had not been there, so Lily had wandered through the chic boutique, had almost gone up to the slender woman at the counter, but had decided against it and left. She had never seriously considered taking a job with Drew Galt, so why had she gone? She needed to see what Drew had offered her, but she'd had no desire to return to the city life.

Where did that leave her? She could close the shop and move back home with her parents. That would be fun. Or she could keep trying to make life work in the yellow cottage. So she braved another day in the shop, and in the evening, she felt restless. She put a few altered shirts into a bag for Paige and decided to walk up to her house to drop them off, as Paige had not been in to pick them up.

Paige lived in one of the original Victorians from the early days of the timber industry. Rows of rose bushes in the garden looked bare and forlorn. The carved wooden sign on the gate read *Williams Residence.*

Lily knocked on the ornate front door, and Paige answered in a floral robe. "Lily! I was just getting ready for bed."

"Sorry to bother you. I needed to get some air."

Paige pushed the hair out of her eyes. "Come on in." She stepped aside and Lily entered the foyer, the smell of chocolate chip cookies wafting into her nose. "Smells good in here."

"I've been baking, a rare occurrence, so take note. I heard what happened."

Lily looked at Paige. "What do you mean, what happened?"

"I know Altona is back."

"Oh." Lily looked at her running shoes. "Small town, nothing private, right?"

"Maybe you should sit down. I'll make you some tea—"

"I brought your alterations." Lily handed the bag to Paige.

"Oh, I should've made it in sooner! I've been so busy."

"No worries. Pay me next time you come in."

"So what are you going to do?" Paige asked.

Lily shrugged. "What is there to do?"

"She's not going to stay. Altona, I mean. She never does. He'll figure it out someday. Takes time."

"Maybe. But . . . I was an idiot to get involved with him."

"No, you weren't," Paige said. "You were only human. He's a good guy. He's just confused."

"I'm confused, too, and I've had enough." Lily glanced into the living room, decorated in plush, opulent furnishings and a lot of floral detail in the frilly curtains. Family photographs crowded the mantel, and a calico cat was curled up on the couch.

"I think he really likes you," Paige went on. "I had lunch with Vanya, and she told me he was upset after you saw him. Moody."

"He was always moody. This really is a small town. I should go—"

"We're not as gossipy as you might think. Okay, we are. The point is, don't give up. I have this terrible feeling that you're going to leave, and we need you here."

Lily's brows rose. "You need me?"

Paige nodded.

"Mommy? Who's at the door?" A tiny boy came down the hall in fire engine pajamas, his dark hair tousled, spots of red and blue paint on his face. The boy from the photo in Paige's wallet.

Paige rested her hand on his head. "Johnny, this is my friend Lily."

"Hello, Johnny," Lily said. "Pleased to meet you."

He rubbed his eyes. "I want milk with the cookies. And a story!"

"I'll see what I can do," Paige said. "Go and wash your face. You've got paint on your cheek."

He looked at Lily, a little wary, then ran down the hall.

"More than one splash with the water!" Paige yelled after him.

"I know!" He disappeared into the bathroom.

"He's living here?" Lily said.

Paige gazed down the hall with fondness. "He's staying here for a few days."

"That's great. I know you wanted more time with him. Well, I should be going."

"Give kitty a pet for me. I owe her for picking out the green dress. Changed my life, and it's not like I get a second chance every day, you know."

"A second chance?"

Paige examined her fingernails, still short. "I've been clean over two years now—"

"Clean?" What on earth was she talking about?

"I did twelve-step, rehab, AA."

"I didn't know." Lily did not see any hint of addiction on Paige's face, in her manner. Were such things always visible?

"That's why I lost Johnny. I didn't have the courage to even try to get him back, but then I met the lawyer at the wedding—"

"That was the guy?"

Paige nodded. "He's helping me . . . It was the dress. He said I looked beautiful in it. I'm never getting rid of it. We'll get married in it. I guess I'm jumping ahead. We're only dating right now."

"Wow, Paige. That's great."

Johnny burst out of the bathroom and came charging down the hall. He leaned against Paige's thigh, still in his pajamas. "Can I have cookies now? I washed my face."

"Let me see, honey." She kneeled and looked into his eyes, cupped his cheeks in her hands. "You look clean, really clean."

He grinned broadly.

"Well, bye," Lily said. "Good to meet you, Johnny!" She hurried down the path.

"We'll be in soon!" Paige called out.

The sky was growing darker, a pale turquoise, and an owl hooted in the trees. Lily thought of Paige at her ex-husband's wedding, resplendent in her altered emerald dress, meeting a new man. Getting her son back, if only temporarily, and pulling herself out of addiction. Perhaps anything was possible, after all.

Chapter Forty

Lily

In the morning, Rupert came in with a tall, well-dressed man and introduced him as Michael.

"I'm pleased to finally meet you," Lily said, and shook Michael's hand.

"I've heard about you," Michael said.

Rupert grinned. "I told Michael all about how you helped me with the suit."

"The one I altered? I just made some minor adjustments."

"More than minor. You altered my whole life."

"Oh, I wouldn't say that." She looked at her shoes.

"You did," Michael said. "Did you know that was the first time Rupert had been back to Virginia since the two of us moved in together? We're talking over a decade. And it took the death of his mother."

"Your mother! I'm so sorry, Rupert. I didn't know."

Rupert took off his gloves and tucked them in his pockets. "Don't worry. I didn't tell you. I told you I needed a suit for a funeral, that's all."

"But it was purple!"

Michael smiled at Rupert. "The perfect color. His parents were none too happy about us, didn't even want to see him again. But he went back. He had the courage."

"I'm sorry," Lily said. "But were you able to reconcile with—?"

"No," Rupert said. "My father still won't talk to me. Neither will my brother."

"But the rest of your family?"

"That's it, father and brother. A few cousins and friends. But it was enough that I went back. Nothing can be perfect. I went to my mom's memorial service and I threw flowers into her grave. Nobody said a word to me. But I said what I needed to say. And I wore a suit that fit me perfectly. It was my color, too."

"Rupert, I . . ." she began.

Rupert looked in the mirror, then at Lily. "I hope you don't leave us. I've been hearing rumors."

She laughed. "What rumors? What have you heard?"

"I teach piano lessons to Bish," Rupert said. "She hadn't been practicing, did a terrible job with her Bach inventions. She mentioned something about you and her dad getting into a fight, and she thinks you're mad at the both of them."

"You teach her piano? Small world," Lily said, shaking her head. "But we didn't get into a fight. I'm not mad at Bish. Her mom came back. Maybe she's got some emotions about that."

Rupert and Michael looked at each other, and then Rupert said, "Her mom came and left. Left being the operative word."

Lily's heart jumped, but why should she care? "Oh, poor Bish. I hear her mom does that a lot, comes and goes."

"I think the 'going' is for good this time," Rupert said, then held up his hands. "Don't take my word for it. I'm just getting that feeling. She moved out a bunch of boxes while I was over there giving Bish her lesson. It was distracting to say the least."

Michael nodded. "Nobody has respect for piano teachers these days."

"Terrible," Lily said, her mind whirling. She couldn't

care, shouldn't care. "If you talk to Bish again, I would like to see her. I'm not mad at her."

"I'll tell her for sure," Rupert said, going over to a black tuxedo. "Our big news is, we're getting married. We've been meaning to come and tell you."

"Married? Wow! I'm happy for you both. Congratulations." Lily hugged each of them in turn.

Rupert took his gloves out of his pockets and put them back on. "We want you to do the clothing."

"Me?" Lily looked around the shop. How could she possibly plan all the outfits for a wedding ceremony?

"We want pictures of us with kitty, too." Rupert picked her up and cradled her.

"But I only have a few tuxedoes and—"

"You've got enough," Rupert said, giving her a knowing look. "We can make it work. You're doing it."

Lily nodded, took a deep breath. "Okay, Rupert, yes, you're right. I'm honored. We can definitely make it work."

Chapter Forty-one

Bish arrived early on Saturday morning, bundled in a new puffy white parka that extended almost to her knees and made her resemble a quilted comforter. In matching winter boots, fuzzy hat, and windstopper gloves, she was equipped to trek to the North Pole. A splash of madrone-colored hair escaped from the hat and formed an unruly frame around her face. Her eyes looked different, older. She wore black-rimmed glasses in a sophisticated style, no longer her bright red frames. Her stance was somehow more grown-up and worldly, too, and Lily imagined her in her twenties, in her thirties, her forties, then stooped and arthritic, her glasses turning into bifocals or trifocals, here in the world and then gone.

Lily resisted the urge to run to Bish and hug her. Not a good idea to hug teenagers. They normally made faces and shrugged you off. So Lily stood behind the counter and tried not to hold her breath. *Thank you, Rupert,* she thought. *You are a true friend.*

Bish pulled off a glove and wiped her nose, and she was back to being sixteen, an excited girl on the threshold of her first Homecoming dance, maybe her first kiss.

She stamped her wet boots on the new welcome mat, the one Lily had found with a cat picture on it and the words "Wipe Your Paws." She tucked her gloves into her pockets and looked up toward the highest shelf in the shop, on which the cat crouched, queen of all she surveyed. "Hey, kitty! I missed you!"

"She missed you, too," Lily said.

Two women browsed the clearance racks, weekend visitors from the city. They looked up briefly and smiled, then returned to browsing, and Lily returned to measuring the sleeves of a red Chanel jacket on the alterations table.

The cat jumped down off the shelves, knocking a stack of scarves to the floor, and rushed over to Bish.

"Whoa, you're growing your coat," Bish said, scooping the cat into her arms. "You would fit in the new winter display in the window."

"It was Rupert's idea," Lily said.

"The snowflakes are a nice touch."

"They don't look too much like dandruff?"

"Looks like kitty got into a box of foam and ripped it to shreds. You could call her Foam. Or Snowflake."

"Not sure about those names," Lily said.

"How about Dandruff? Or Fluff?"

"Not sure about those, either. Rupe says that white fluff is some newfangled biodegradable material."

"Yeah, like newfangled recycled paper. Cool Radio Flyer."

"We didn't have a sled, but the red wagon is vintage, so I improvised."

"I like that, improvising." Bish put the cat down and strolled through the shop, her boots clopping on the hardwood. She took in the lighting, the rearranged carousels, the mixture of the old and the new. Her gaze passed over the mannequins and hat racks, cat trees, and scratching posts.

"I was going to stop by sooner," she said, "but . . . Whoa, you've got a lot more stuff in here now." She gravitated toward the alterations table and looked around at the clutter—scraps of fabric, piles of men's neckties, pins and scissors, sewing machine, spools of thread.

"I can't stay on top of the mess . . ." Lily began.

"It's a good kind of mess. A lived-in kind of mess. Sort of like my bedroom. Except my mom always wants to clean it up, drives me insane."

"Did you have a good time with her?" Might as well get to the point. "Looks as though she succeeded in keeping you warm. Did she buy the parka?"

"The whole shebang." Bish looked down at her new Arctic-worthy boots. "She got on my dad's case, said he had no sense of fashion and dressed me like a vagabond. Then she went overboard taking me shopping. It's a guilt thing."

"What do you mean, a guilt thing?"

Bush unzipped her coat and took off her new knit cap, her hair sticking up in a halo of static. "It's what absent parents do. They feel guilty about not being around for their kids, so they buy them off."

Lily rolled up the tape measure and set it on the table. "You're too wise for your years, you know that? Where did you learn about parental guilt? From Dr. Phil, or was it Oprah?"

"Oprah's not on regular daytime TV anymore. Where have you been?"

"Obviously not watching TV."

"I don't either. But I can picture the show, 'Absent Parents on a Guilt Trip and the Kids They Buy Off.' Some parents buy their kids, like, entire houses or islands. I get the clothes, but I don't mind the guilt thing. I like it when my mom buys me stuff, plus she buys stuff for my friends, too. But I wish she wouldn't pretend. It's so lame."

"Pretend what? That she loves you? She does love you. She does the best she can. We all do." Why was Lily apologizing for Bish's itinerant mother?

"She loves me in her own way, I guess. But she doesn't like to hang around and make Halloween costumes and cookies. She's not that kind of mom, but I've come to terms with how she is. Took me a while, but I grew out of needing her motherly love. As we get older, we get over things. I'm not a kid anymore."

"As you get older, huh?" Lily pressed her lips together to keep from smiling. She could hear the sadness beneath Bish's words. "You're ancient. So old and wise, I'm surprised you haven't developed cataracts."

"Come on." Bish slapped Lily's arm playfully. "So what is that jacket on the table? Cool gold buttons."

"Chanel logos on each one, see? CC. Red wool. It's lined with matching red silk on the inside. Sometimes these Chanel jackets can run upwards of eight thousand dollars. But I'm selling it for much less."

"Are you going to alter it?"

Lily stepped back and looked at the jacket, admiring its delicate seams and pockets. "Some things are perfect just the way they are. The key is knowing which ones to change, and which ones to leave untouched."

"And this one you're leaving alone."

"Exactly. Like your parka, too. Fits you perfectly. Your mom has good taste."

"Yeah, I guess. But I look like a walking igloo."

"No, the white suits you. Did you find a good Homecoming dress?"

"We looked all over. My mom likes to shop. She buys stuff for herself all the time, too. We ended up with this designer dress, like, so expensive. Tadashi Shoji or something."

"Sounds lovely."

"It has these ruffles stuck on it. It comes with a transparent cape in case I get cold."

"That's great. I bet you're so glad you, um, went shopping with her. So, what about shoes?"

"Kate Spade New York Charmers."

Lily glanced at her rows of secondhand designer shoes. "So you had a productive visit."

"The dress fits me, but I can't walk in the shoes. I was just humoring my mom. I couldn't let her down. She got this look on her face. She came into the fitting room and looked in the mirror and got all teary-eyed. And the sales lady came in and went on and on about how I look like my mom and we're both so pretty and—how can I look like my mom when I'm not like her at all? We have totally different personalities. I'm way more like my dad."

"I'm sure you have elements of both parents. You're ambitious like your mother, aren't you? You do well in school, you have big plans. You don't give up."

"But I don't wear ruffles and frills. I feel like a doily in that dress. Guys will want to put their drinks on me, not dance with me!"

"I'm sure it's not that bad. If your mom thought you looked beautiful, she was telling the truth."

"Her version of beautiful. But the dress is not me. I'm not fluffy. I'm not like the cat. She's naturally fluffy. It's who she is. But I'm not, and I'm so not Dolte and Cabana!" She took off the glasses and waved them around, squinting.

"You mean Dolce & Gabbana," Lily said. "Is that what those glasses are? Your mom got those for you, too?"

"They keep slipping down." She propped them back on her nose and took an exaggerated, deep breath.

"Your other glasses keep slipping down your nose, too. Both pairs look good on you, if it helps at all."

Bish shrugged. "So did you sell the Cinderella dress then?"

"Oh no, I haven't sold it. I made a few final changes and then I, uh, hung it up back here in the closet. I'm not sure what I'm going to do with it yet."

Bish's eyes brightened. "Can I see it?"

Lily brought it out of the closet, the blue silk shimmering as it caught the light.

Bish drew in an audible breath. "This is the dress? This is what you did?"

"Just a few adjustments."

"Are you kidding? Can I try it on?"

"If you want. I'm not offended if you wear the dress you bought with your mom. Honestly. Don't worry about hurting my feelings."

But Bish didn't seem to hear. She was already on her way to the fitting room. The cat trotted over to sit near the three-way mirror in her usual spot.

Bish emerged looking like the brightest star in the Milky Way. "You're truly beautiful," Lily said.

Bish pressed her hands to her cheeks. She extended her leg, revealing a little thigh, the split in the dress just high enough to be tantalizing but not too revealing. "I love this. I love it so much. I want to wear this one. What do you think, kitty?"

The cat reached out to touch the shimmering skirt

with her paw, claws retracted. Then she sat back and squinted.

"See? She loves it, too."

The other shoppers were looking at Bish now.

"But what about your Tadashi Shoji dress?" Lily said. "You should wear it, especially if your mom spent a lot of money on it."

"She won't know if I don't wear it to the dance. I'll take a picture of myself in it and send her the photo."

"Bish!"

"She won't be here. She's already gone. She's on a plane somewhere, like Paris, who knows?"

"I'm sorry she's gone again."

"Yeah, whatever." Bish pulled back, a touch of sadness in her eyes but also resignation. "I'm going to need help with my makeup and hair, the whole shebang."

"I'll help you. Are you going on a date to the dance, or—?"

"This guy who plays saxophone in the school band. He's really cool. He's going to pick me up in a limo with my best friend and her boyfriend."

"That's fabulous. I'm so happy for you. Um, will your Kate Spade shoes go with the blue dress?"

"I'll have to come back with them." Bish turned to

examine the scooped back of the dress. Her reflection in triplicate, with the cat at her feet, would remain in Lily's mind forever.

Then Bish flung her arms around Lily's neck and hugged her. "This is the most beautiful dress in the history of the entire universe."

"Um, thanks," Lily said, relishing Bish's teenage tendency to speak in extremes. "I'm happy for you, the happiest I've been in the history of the entire universe."

Bish pulled back and smiled. "So, like, I want you to meet my friends. Can we all go out for pizza? Or can we stop by here on our way to the dance?"

"Absolutely."

"I'll introduce you as my dad's girlfriend. Is that okay?"

Lily felt her face flushing hot. "But—"

"It's true, isn't it? Are you going to marry my dad? Move in with us?"

"Maybe you should introduce me as your friend. I am your friend, Bish. I'll always be your friend."

"I know, but I'm not the kind of person to beat around the bush. And I want you to be my dad's girlfriend, anyway. When he talks about you, he smiles. He's like nicer to me. You should marry him."

"I'm not even seeing your dad."

"I'm just saying." Bish narrowed her gaze at Lily. "You need to go over and see him."

"Let's take it all one step at a time. I don't think I can do that—"

"Yes, you can. He's working late tonight."

"You want me to go and see him at the clinic."

Bish nodded. "Go and talk to him. He really wants to talk to you."

"I can't go to the clinic tonight, Bish."

"Why not? I already told him you would go there around eight."

"But, Bish—"

"Awesome!" She went back into the dressing room, came out in her white quilted getup and handed Lily the blue dress on its padded hanger. "Can you keep it here for now? I'll come back later with the shoes."

"I can't wait." Lily dared to look forward with hope, to the next visit with Bish, the next cozy night with the cat.

On her way out the door, Bish looked back and said, "Don't forget—the clinic tonight at eight. Be there or be square."

Chapter Forty-two

Lily

Lily considered working right through the evening, ignoring Bish's request. But as the afternoon wore on, the minutes seemed to pass too slowly, and against her better judgment, her heart began to flutter with anticipation. She took too long to get dressed at seven thirty, to fuss with her hair. What was she doing, going to the clinic? What did Ben want to tell her? Maybe he would apologize for leading her on, or thank her for Bish's dress, or maybe he had something to tell her about the cat.

At the clinic, she found the front door unlocked, but

the reception area was dark and empty. The familiar, faint scent of pine cleaner drifted into her nose, and a diffused, squarish light spilled in from the hallway.

"Ben? Are you here? It's me, Lily!"

"Lily?" Ben came up front in his lab coat, looking worried. But he couldn't hide the trace of excitement in his eyes when he saw her. "What are you doing here? Is the cat all right? Did she collapse again?"

"The cat is fine." She was breathless. "Bish told me to come. She said you wanted to talk to me."

"She said that, did she? Come on in." Ben took off his lab coat and led her into his office. Underneath the coat, he wore jeans and a white T-shirt.

He sat at his desk and rubbed his temples. "It's been a long day. Have a seat." He gestured toward an extra chair, but Lily remained standing. The photograph on his desk was gone.

"So?" She crossed her arms over her chest. "What did you want to talk to me about?"

He looked up at her. "I didn't ask Bish to tell you anything. If I'd wanted to talk to you, I would've called you myself."

She turned to leave, her heart pounding. "Sorry, then I was mistaken."

"Wait!" In a moment, he was up, coming around from

behind the desk to stand in front of Lily. "I'm glad you came here. You didn't return my calls."

"I'm not sure what we have to say to each other." Her throat closed, but she couldn't cry in front of Ben again.

"Lily, I—I'm sorry about what happened. But Altona and I—we had a long history. It's over now."

"Until the next time?"

"What about you? The shadow of Josh is always with you."

"Josh died. He's gone." Her mouth felt dry—her eyes, her skin, everything. The room was too cluttered, oppressive. "Would you mind if I step outside for a minute? I need some air."

"Walk with me out to the pier. The salty sea air might do us good. I'll lock up."

"I don't know. I should get back."

"Lily, please, grant me this one walk."

She nodded, he grabbed his coat, and they headed out into the cold night, the black sky punctuated by the glint of stars. The quaint town of Fairport looked magical in the moonlight, the shop window displays dimly lit.

"How's Bish?" Lily asked. "How is she taking her mother's latest departure?"

"Final departure," he said. "She's not the type to stay. She never was. Bish is taking it as well as she can."

"I'm sorry, Ben." She was genuinely sorry for him.

"It's possible to have regrets, but also to know it wasn't right. I could never be with her again."

"Are you sure?"

"Would you be with your husband again if you could?"

"We had a great love."

He nodded as if he understood. "But he's gone, and Altona's gone. We've got to move forward. Life keeps going."

She nodded, too, her eyes filling with tears.

A few seagulls sat on the wooden railing, chattering softly. The tide was high, water engulfing the pilings, swallowing the beach and lapping the rocks near the road.

"Wait, just a minute." Lily stopped halfway along the pier, resting her arms on the wooden railing, and peered down into the water. "I love it here. I can breathe on the island. I went back to the city, thinking maybe I could run away again, but I can't."

Ben stood beside her, his presence comforting and something more, too. "So where is home for you?"

"The island feels like the place I want to be. I still have a lot of work to do, to figure out my life."

"You'll make it. You're a survivor."

"Thanks. I hope you're right." She turned her face to the wind, and she thought of the fun she'd had with Ben.

Maybe they would go out again. Why not? The lights of Seattle winked in the distance—a view to another world.

Did Josh reside in another world, too? In Heaven? In an afterworld similar to Earth? She could not know, but she no longer sensed him nearby. He had gained some distance from her, like a boat drifting away on the waves. *Good-bye, Joshua*, she thought. *Smooth sailing.*

She reached behind her neck and unclasped the gold chain, then she gathered the necklace in a bundle, the wedding ring and vial of ash both in the palm of her hand now, all that she had left of him. She dropped the wedding ring into her pocket, and then she opened the vial, turned it upside down, and let the wind whisk the ashes away into the sea.

Chapter Forty-three

Kitty

I love springtime in Fairport. Everything sparkles, a touch of magic in the air. Flowers bloom in bursts of bright color, butterfly bushes spill over with yellow spray, and tiny birds twitter in the trees. I dream about catching a nice, plump specimen, but then again, I prefer to remain indoors. I've had enough of the dangerous outdoor life.

I've spent the last two hours sitting in a sun spot in the window, gazing out at the people, the passing clouds, and the slope leading down to the beach. Lily's shop sign still swings in the breeze, but she changed the name from Past

Perfect to Luna's Corner. She named me Bella Luna, meaning "beautiful moon." She said I was her light in the darkness.

She still talks to me all the time. I can't escape the monologues, but these days, she chatters about Ben and Bish, her next clothing project, and some design contest she's entering. I can see her future in the dust motes catching the light, in the angle of the sun, in the smile on Ben's face when he stops by. Sometimes all three of them—Ben, Bish, and Lily—go out together. When they come back inside, bringing the smells of the world, they tell me stories and give me treats and love.

The spirit of Josh has gone away, don't ask me where. And the angry, inky ghost finally found her lost sailor, who whisked her away on his phantom ship. Sometimes new spirits flit through the shop or linger in the clothes, but they soon wander off.

One afternoon, Vanya strides in with a bundle in some kind of a sling.

"Is this little Sven?" Lily says, rushing over to look inside the sling. "He's gorgeous!"

"Seven pounds, eight ounces," Vanya says. A baby? A human one? I lick my paw.

"I'm so happy for you," Lily says, taking the baby from Vanya and cradling the creature in her arms.

"I was wondering if you would be Sven's godmother. Kind of like an auntie. He doesn't have any aunties, only uncles."

Lily looks up and smiles. "Of course, I would love to. It would be my honor."

"Do you have baby clothes?"

"We carry a few items in the back. Oh, look! Luna wants to see."

"I like that name, Luna," Vanya says. "Lily and Luna. You make a good pair."

"Her full name is Bella Luna."

"Even better."

Somehow, I ended up between Lily and Vanya, looking up at the human infant all swaddled in white. I'm reaching up, too, standing on my hind legs.

Lily kneels to show me the tiny, hairless human, its face squished and pink, but it smells good, like milk and sweetness. Hard to believe this squirming bundle will become a full-grown person. I touch his forehead with my nose.

"Aw, how cute. Luna likes him. He's adorable, isn't he?" Lily kisses the baby's cheek. What about me?

As if Lily has heard my thoughts, she hands the baby back to Vanya and bends to pick me up. Bliss, comfort. "You're adorable, too," she says, and puts me down again.

Vanya points to the shimmering white gown on the

mannequin by the window. "That's a lovely dress. Have I seen that one before?"

"I was repairing the bodice," Lily says, looking at the gown. "That was my wedding dress."

"Yours! You must've been beautiful in it."

Lily smiles a little and sighs, her eyes bright with tears, her heartbeat steady and hopeful.

ACKNOWLEDGMENTS

Many thanks to my agent, Kevan Lyon; my editor, Wendy McCurdy; Katherine Pelz; Leslie Gelbman, publisher of Berkley Books; and all the talented people at Berkley; as well as my longtime writing group buddies—Susan Wiggs, Sheila Roberts, Elsa Watson, and Kate Breslin. Thanks to my story coach, Michael Hauge.

Thanks to Stephanie Lile and Bryan Sabol, and my Friday Tea group friends including, but not limited to, Toni Bonnell, Carol Caldwell, Dianne Gardner, Theo Gustafson, Catherine Hickey, Sandi Hill, Terrel Hoffman, Elizabeth Corcoran Murray, Penny Percenti, Gwynn Rogers, Pat Stricklin, Jan Symonds, Dee Marie, and Carol Wissmann. What would I do without my swimming friends, author Lois Faye Dyer and retired bookseller Rose Marie Harris?

Thanks to Maple Grove Cottage, a new and used designer

and vintage clothing store in Poulsbo, Washington; Aimee McWhorter-Compton; Pretty Parlor in Seattle, including Angelica Gehm, clothing designer with her own label, Kombat Glamour; and the two resident shop cats, Vincent and Petunia. Like Bella Luna, Petunia has one blue eye and one green eye. I'm grateful to the shop owner, Anna Lange, as well.

Thanks so much to Andrea Hurst and her Coupeville writing posse, including Rowena Williamson, for their feedback and knowledge. Thanks, Deb Lund and Michele Torrey; thanks to the Garden Isle Guest Cottages in Coupeville; to Matthew Sias for his thoughtful feedback on early versions of the first chapters. Anjana Gattani, I appreciate your cat stories. Thanks to Bill Larson and Carol Ann Morris, Anita LaRae, Christa Sherwood, and Judy Hart. Marilyn Lundberg, deepest thanks for your insight and support. Thanks to Chief Wayne Senter, and I appreciate the staff at the Gig Harbor Public Library for giving me a quiet place in which to work. Thanks to Hedgebrook for giving me the cat's voice in Waterfall Cottage—and Meadow House for a weekend.

Thanks to my family, including my husband, Joseph. To write the kitty's character, I needed help from the kitties I've loved and lost—Shanti, Monet, and Alex—and those still living with us and entertaining us nonstop: Cheyenne, Ruby, Simon, Teddy, and our own Bella Luna.

Read on for a special preview of
another charming novel from Anjali Banerjee

Haunting Jasmine

Available now from Berkley Books

Chapter One

I didn't see this turn of events coming, or going. My ex-husband, Rob, used his charm like a weapon, and ultimately he didn't care whose heart he broke—or whose life he ruined. Neither did he care whose bed he woke up in. My mother would say, *Well, Jasmine, that's an American penis for you. You should've married a Bengali. Faithful, good, and true to his culture.* Her words conjure an image of the royal Bengali penis decked out in a traditional *churidar kurta*, its head peeking from the gold-embroidered white silk outfit at our traditional Indian wedding. But my mother won't get her wish—I won't marry again.

Now that the divorce is final, I need a break from L.A., from the errant ex-husband whom I once thought was perfect. I'm alone on the ferry to Shelter Island, a green dot of rain-soaked darkness in the middle of Puget Sound. Out on the boat's breezeway, the wind whips my hair, reminding me that I'm still alive, that I can still feel the cold. Robert's number pops up on my cell phone screen—the green digits that I have come to loathe. I ignore the call and send him into the barren wasteland of Voice Mail. Let him deal with the real estate agent and the vultures descending on the condo. I've made my temporary escape into solitude.

As we approach the island, the eastern shoreline emerges from a wall of fog. Madrone and fir trees tumble down to wild rocky beaches; forested hillsides rise into pewter skies; and the town of Fairport hugs the harbor in a density of antique buildings and twinkling lights. My heartbeat thuds. What am I doing here? Soon the moss will grow between my fingers, in the creases of my nose, and in the pockets of my thin raincoat, where I keep Auntie's letter, her urgent request that summoned me home.

In the age of e-mail, she prefers to write the old-fashioned way. I pull her note from its hiding place and sniff the paper—a faint scent of rose. Each time I unfold the letter, the fragrance changes. Yesterday it was sandal-wood, the day before, jasmine. But the words remain the same, written in Auntie's slanted golden script:

I must go to India. I need you to run the bookstore while I'm away. Only you will do.

When I called her to ask, *Why me?* she mentioned "fixing her health" in Kolkata. She wouldn't say more, but how could I deny my fragile old auntie? She promised me refuge among the classics, although I haven't had time to read a novel in years. The evidence hides in my oversized handbag—a rolled-up copy of *Forbes* magazine and a cell phone, a BlackBerry, and a netbook. The weight of technology pulls on the shoulder strap. I barely have room for the usual supplies—compact, lipstick, tissue, aspirin, allergy pills, charge cards, receipts, and a bundle of keys, including one that opens the exercise room at the office. Not a single novel, and yet, what do I have to lose? How hard can it be to sell the latest Nora Roberts or Mary Higgins Clark?

A month on the island, sitting in the bookstore, is a small enough sacrifice for my beloved auntie. I brought work to keep me occupied, including a roll of green bar reports that I haven't had time to review.

As the ferry docks, a gust of wind snatches Auntie's letter from my hand. The pink paper flutters into the water, and for a moment her handwriting glows in the evening light, then dissolves into sparkles as the letter sinks. I consider diving in after it—drowning would be a welcome release from sorrow. But a seagull calls out, admonishing me to keep my chin up, to defy Rob.

I square my shoulders and join the herd of passengers shuffling down the ramp to Harborside Road. Lined with cast-iron lampposts and giant old poplar trees, the street meanders along the waterfront and disappears into a silver mist. I imagine entering that mist and emerging in a new world where men don't have affairs, where two people can rewind time, fall in love again, and not hurt each other, but I know this is impossible. Time moves in one direction. I must keep up the pace toward Auntie's bookstore, although my heels were not made for brick sidewalks and my coat is too thin for the weather.

The town hasn't changed in the year since I last visited. Classic Cycle, Fairport Chiropractic, Island Eye Care. One token business for each human need. If you want a selection from which to choose, you're out of luck. A handwritten Rotary Bake Sale sign flaps in the window of the Fairport Café, where neighbors gather to share gossip and recipes.

I can't remember when I last had time to crack open a

cookbook. In L.A., Rob and I subsisted on takeout, a secret that would annoy my mother. She believes every good Bengali daughter should be like my sister, Gita, who excels at preparing curried fish. I barely remember how to boil water. Now that I'll be staying with my parents, I'll have a harder time hiding my flaws.

I set off toward Auntie's bookstore, six blocks north at the water's edge—a three-story Queen Anne Victorian painted in burnt umber and white. As I approach the house, a little girl runs out the front door, crying, followed by her mother.

"But I wanted *Curious George!*" the little girl wails.

". . . next time," her mother says and bundles her into a Volkswagen Beetle.

I stop at the curb in front of the bookstore, my heartbeat kicking up. I'm not prepared for screaming children. And I forgot how large the house is, and how complex—a pattern of bay windows, turrets, and a wraparound porch. Close up, patches of disrepair come into stark relief. The paint is peeling on the railing; a few shingles have come loose on the roof. Auntie should renovate, repaint, and place a neon sign in the window.

I take a deep breath and drag my suitcase up the narrow steps to the back door, which is now the main entrance to the bookstore. A well-worn path leads around the house to the ornate front door facing the waterfront, recalling a bygone era when important guests arrived by sea. Now I doubt anyone important ever crosses the threshold.

As I push open the back door, soft voices float toward me. The words coalesce, then change their minds and drift away. Inside the foyer, I'm submerged in dimness, save the faint orange glow from a Tiffany lamp. I'll add a few bright lights to this entryway.

The heavy door slams behind me, shutting out the world. The lemon scent of furniture polish rises through the dust; the air hangs heavy with the smell of mothballs. I can't survive a month in this stuffiness, among useless antiques and out-of-print titles.

And the clutter. Auntie leaves no surface uncovered. To my left, a dusty Kashmiri carpet hangs on the wall, depicting the tree of life in subtle shades of red and gold. As I step closer, the colors shift to green and yellow. Perhaps the light has changed, or perhaps the Hindu elephant-headed god, Ganesh, is playing a trick on me. He sits to my right, a brass statue waiting to frighten customers away. Auntie should display bestsellers here, not statues.

But before I can stop myself, I reach out to rub Ganesh's enormous belly. He will curse me for not kneeling to touch his feet. After all, he is powerful, temperamental, and unpredictable.

"Maybe you could curse Rob, make his penis fall off," I whisper to Ganesh. He does not reply.

I leave my luggage next to him and nearly bump into a man who seems to have materialized from nowhere. I look up into a rugged face, shadowed eyes, dark, windswept hair. A faint blue glow shines behind him, accentuating his silhouette. He's dressed for leisure in a hooded travel jacket, brown cargo pants, and hiking boots. He's carrying a pile of books under one arm. Apparently he has a lot of time for reading.

"That would hurt," he says. His voice resonates—a deep baritone that ripples across my skin. He gives off the scents of pine trees and fresh air.

"What would hurt?" I can't get past him. He's in my way, and he shows no signs of moving.

"Losing the family jewels."

"Oh, you heard what I said." The blood rises in my cheeks.

"Glad I'm not this Rob guy." A ghost of a smile touches his lips. He's mocking me.

"Believe me, if you were Robert, you'd be dead." I try to slip past him and nearly stumble on a snag in the carpet.

He steps aside. "You're in such a hurry."

"I move at regular speed. I'm not on island time."

His gaze is steady, unabashed. "Where are you from?"

"L.A. I'm here to help my aunt . . . temporarily." I need a hot shower, a cup of espresso.

"Your aunt. That lovely lady in the sari."

"One and the same." So she still attracts the attention of younger men. And she still wears saris.

"Beauty must run in the family," he says.

My ears heat up. I'm glad they're hiding beneath my hair. I haven't felt beautiful in a long time. "You're bold, aren't you, Mr.—?"

"Hunt. Connor Hunt. And you must be Jasmine."

"How do you know my name?"

"I heard your aunt talking about you. She made you sound intriguing."

Me, intriguing? I've never been intriguing. "You heard my aunt gossiping about me? What did she say? I need to have a word with her."

"She said you'll be working for her."

"That's it? That's not intriguing."

"She said you were running away."

"Me, running?" My voice rises, and a knot is forming in the back of my neck. "That's none of your business, and I'm not running. Just to set the record straight."

He raises his hand. "No problem there."

"I have a lot of work to catch up on, so if you don't mind, I should find my aunt."

"Do you have time for coffee? Or tea?"

I can't believe this guy. "I won't have time for dating while I'm here." *Especially not with men like you. Men who come on to strangers. Men like Robert.*

"Who said anything about a date?" He steps closer, and I step back.

"What would you call it then? Do you always come on to women in bookstores?"

"Only to you. I can't change your mind?"

"Not a chance." I want to shove him out the front door. He's exactly like Robert, who probably flirted with every female he encountered. I'm not going this route again. I've become the fortified castle of Jasmine.

He rubs his forefinger across his eyebrow. "I can't lie. I'm disappointed. But I hope to see you later." He slips out the door and disappears into the blustery evening.

Chapter Two

Good riddance.

The nerve of him, making a pass at a stranger. I bet he's got a wife stashed at home, maybe kids, too.

When Robert first met Lauren, did he smile so innocently and ask her on a date? Did he slide the wedding band off his finger, drop it in his pocket? Did he pretend he cared about her?

Men are driven by testosterone. They think they can get any woman they want. But nobody will get me, ever again. I need to call in to the office, make sure the company hasn't canned anyone else. Make sure I have a job to which I can return.

I hang my coat in the hall closet and slip into the cluttered room to my right. I hold up my BlackBerry at all angles. I check down one aisle, then another. No signal.

A loud snoring emanates from the History aisle labeled WORLD WAR II. A bearded man has fallen asleep in an armchair, a book about battleships facedown on his chest. Amazing how some people have so much time to sleep, to read. Don't they have work to do? E-mails to check?

"Bippy, my dearest niece!" Auntie exclaims behind me in a voice far bigger than her size. She has always called me by my baby nickname.

"Auntie!" I whip around, and she rushes toward me, arms outstretched. She's as spritely as a teenage girl, yet her paper-white hair, deeply wrinkled face, and silver-rimmed bifocals betray her age. Her knitted reindeer sweater clashes with her green chiffon sari. She shows no trace of her mystery illness.

"Why didn't you say you'd arrived?" She envelops me in a hug filled with her particular spicy scent, the scent of Auntie, and a touch of Pond's cold cream. Childhood memories flood back to me, of Auntie making curried cauliflower and the sweet yogurt dessert *mishti doi*; handing me brand-new copies of *Curious George, Winnie the Pooh* . . . Did I ever actually read those silly books?

I gaze into her eyes, searching for a hint of what ails her. "I was looking for you. How are you?"

"I'm holding up, thank the gods."

The guy in the armchair snores louder.

A man rushes into the room in a haze of irritation. He's dressed in autumn colors, black hair teased and oiled. He probably spends an hour in front of the mirror every morning, primping and coiffing. He exudes delicate, elegant charm, his features rounded as if sculpted by the weather.

"Ruma, the window display is messed up again, and I am sick of fixing it." He glances at the snoring man and shakes his head. "Weekend warriors are starting early, and it's only Monday."

"Weekend warriors?" I say.

The man glances at me. "The loungers, the sleepers!"

"You don't get too many of those, do you?"

"Where have you been, honey?" He looks me up and down. "Oh, you must be Jasmine."

"Pleased to meet you," I say, wondering what Auntie has told him about me.

"This is Tony," Auntie says. "You'll be working with him while I'm away."

I smile to hide the jumping beans in my gut. "Looking forward to it," I say politely.

Tony shakes my hand so tightly, my bones nearly break. "So you're moving in."

I let go of his hand. "I'm only visiting. I'll be staying with my parents a few blocks away."

Tony's mouth opens into a round O. "Oh, no, you won't. You need to hold down the fort. That means you stay here."

I turn to my aunt. "Is he serious?"

"Of course. That's part of the deal. You must be a care-taker for the house."

"I can't stay. I'll spend the nights at Ma and Dad's, in the guest room. I need a desk for my work, a table. Your attic apartment is too small."

"Ah, but it's the best spot in the house."

"But Ma has the extra bedroom made up. Lots of space there."

"Out of the question. You must be here, in case the toilets act up . . ."

"The toilets?" I'm not a plumber.

". . . or there's a power failure or, gods forbid, a fire."

"A fire?!"

"We've got extinguishers. And we have many evening and early morning events. So you see, you have to stay—"

"Events?" I blink. What events could she possibly host in this remote corner of the world?

"Wednesday morning we've got an author coming to sign her books, quite early—"

"Can't Tony come in?"

"I live in Seattle," Tony says, frowning. "I take the ferry. Usually only on weekdays, but I'll be here this weekend to help you out."

Auntie pats my arm. "You see? Tony is dedicated. Bookselling is a lifestyle, not a job. You don't expect to arrive when the store opens and leave when it closes, do you?" Her eyebrows rise like two silver suspension bridges.

"Actually, I do." My handbag is slipping off my shoulder. I hastily pull up the strap.

Tony is chuckling. I want to slap him.

Auntie waggles a bejeweled forefinger in front of my face. "This is the nature of running the bookstore. Working after hours. Sleeping in the attic, listening to the books breathing at night."

"Books . . . breathing?" I hope not. My aunt needs to clean the rooms, open the windows, install more lights, and order in the new bestsellers.

"Full-time job, nah?" she says.

"But I have a lot of work to do while I'm here, for my

real . . . my *other* job, and I'm wondering about the cell phone signal."

"You won't find one here." She gives me a warm smile, then turns to Tony. "She's so busy, you know. She helps people sock away their money for retirement."

"In socially responsible accounts," I say. *And if I don't make a perfect presentation to the Hoffman Company when I return to L.A., I may be out of a job.*

Tony looks me up and down again. "Girl, you know how to dress, but those threads are for the city, not here. You can't wear those heels to work. Your feet will start hurting."

My toes are already sore. "I have a pair of sneakers in my suitcase."

"Then wear them. And you have jeans, I hope?"

"Only one pair."

He rolls his eyes. "You'll be doing a lot of laundry, unless you buy another pair of jeans. You're going to be on your feet all day."

"I thought I might help at the checkout register—"

Tony guffaws. "What rock have you been hiding under?"

"I've been living in the real world."

He throws his head back and laughs. "You call L.A. the real world?"

I bite my lip to keep from spouting an acerbic reply. The snoring man snores louder. A bulb flickers on the ceiling, the floor squeaks, and a cloud of dust wafts by. I break into a fit of sneezing. The next few weeks are going to crawl by at a slug's pace.